Wicked Pleasures™

SEXIBITION

Author: Mikeal Martin

ISBN: 1-892779-01-3

Printed by Cedar Publishing, 1117 First Avenue SE, Cedar Rapids, Iowa 52402, 1-800-301-4545

This book is dedicated to

Francesca

Thank you for believing in me.

TABLE OF CONTENTS

Introduction

In the forum of African-American Erotica, the mainstream publishers have ignored the true essence of who we are as a people. Most of the books available to us are toned down with abstract ideas of sexuality. In response to this literary censorship I have written

Wicked Pleasures: SEXIBITION.

This is my statement, these are my thoughts,
and this is now your book.
Enjoy.

Wicked

WICKED PLEASURES

Every twisted perversion,
With each other we will share.
Wicked Pleasures are immoral,
But lust for flesh, doesn't care.

Erotic Words are so convincing,
As resistance has no voice.
Your *minds* will weigh the options,
But your *organs* will make the choice.

Desires rage in Anarchy,
As your morals will just watch in awe.
Because *Wicked Pleasures* are now *sexual government*,
And *Satisfaction*, is now martial law!

Winds of sin will blow your mind,
Your bank of values, depleted of funds.
Lust, is the assassin of good judgement,
AS SOMETHING WICKED
THIS WAY COMES.

Assante Daydreamer

Assante Daydreamer

What Goes Up, Must Come Down

When a young man comes of age, and is capable of reproduction, his body has a unique, yet unforgettable way to signal him. This signal changes his life from that moment on. After the signal has been delivered, for most of this young man's life, he will think about sex almost every hour of every day, for the rest of his life. This signal, as we all know, is called the "wet dream," the proverbial start of it all. However, there are two sides to every story, two sides to every coin. Instead of thinking about the great "head" men get in that dream...this is a story about the one never spoken of...the great piece of "tail". What about her?

That's right, what about the woman in the dream? The ultimate woman. The woman that we are genetically programmed to lust after. The exotic flame that leads the moth. For many, this is the first woman we are intimate with. For many, this is the woman we subconsciously are out there looking for. But what if she had a life? What would she be looking for? Have you ever wondered...what if the woman we all dream about, the woman that is without a doubt, our perfect sexual mate...what if she were real?

Well she is. Her name is Assante. She is an occupant in the dreamscape. An *employee* to our lust. She was created with the sole purpose of being the perfect sexual mate to every man *or* woman who lusts for a female. What makes her so perfect? Assante has the ability to read the minds of all that cross her path. She can make love, have sex, or fuck millions of men or women at once, feeling all of them as an individual experience. She can assume any female form, and manipulate her body in any fashion. Above and beyond all else, she can feel what we feel. She was created with the very special ability to actually feel the sexual excitement and pleasure that she delivers to others. Every stroke, every lick, the racing of the heart, the tingling and twitching of our nerves and muscles; she can feel it all. She has to, how else can she best serve us? This is an intricate tool in her work, in her servitude. Her total existence in the dream scape is one of service to others. She is there for us when we sleep. She is there for all who need her. But what happens when she goes to sleep? Who is there for her? The answer to that question is, us.

That's right. When we sleep, she serves us. But when she sleeps, we serve her, in a way. After Assante fulfills all the fantasies of the night, she lays her head down and slips into her dream scape, which we commonly call the real world! Where else would a being of dreams drift off to in her sleep? Seems easy enough to understand, right? We dream, we go to her; she dreams, she comes to us. No problem, right? Wrong! Assante spends all her waking hours in servitude! In her dream, in our reality, she is free to be served. Armed with all the abilities of her blessed creation, she walks amongst us in the day, knowing each and every one of us. Remembering what we called on her to do in our most graphic of dreams, in our most sacred of perversions. In some cases she walks by men, and remembers the times she was their loving wife, pampered in exotic places, worshiped as the perfect woman; and by women to whom she was the most gentle and caressing woman in their lives. Loving how the innocent, confused young women, struggling to identify their sexuality, would just let go, and melt with her, inside of her, she cherished those tender moments. But those are, sadly, the minority. She is out, in most cases, for payback. Which is just fine with her, because with her limited time in our realm, she carries a curse. In the dream scape she can do no wrong, it's part of her abilities, that all she does will be right for the dreamers. In our reality, it's the exact opposite, anyone she has sex with, will have their lives turn for the worst. It's her burden to bear; with great power comes great responsibility. So she targets the sick, the men and women that make her reality a nightmare, while they dream. She has the memories of the little men, dreaming of their big dicks! Literally tearing her in half! She can feel how their orgasms would build greater and greater, as she cried more and more. What was this inane need to hurt her, to rip her apart? And the women, with altered visions of the size of their breasts, and with a pussy flowing so hard it would drown her, and often did. How she felt their sense of power while they smothered her, making her serve them, eat them, suck them, in total servitude, never giving back. Oh yes, all the times she had been raped by sick men in their dreams, by child molesters requiring that she were to be a little girl, innocent and tender, just so they could rape and sodomize her. The times when the mentally deranged chopped up her body, mutilated her, dissected her, and came in her dead mouth. Assante has seen the best and the worst of us, she has lived through it, and she is one of us. Now, we have to deal with HER.

Assante's dreams begin at the break of dawn, she has until dusk to be amongst the real. A favorite place for her to frequent is Venice Beach, California. Here, in the summer, she finds many men and women that she remembers as particularly perverted, a cornucopia of sexual deviation. She stands next to the boardwalk, looking for her next sexual conquest. As the passersby see her, they all turn their heads in disbelief. This is a common reaction, for they all see a different woman. The guy in the toga, skating with the radio, sees her as a 5'4" Nigerian woman, with brown eyes, and a humble, submissive stance. The blond body builder sees her as a 6-foot blond woman with incredible muscle definition, and huge breasts. All of the on-lookers see her as a different woman, all see her as their perfect sexual conquest. The only people that have any sort of immunity to her power are those that have no sexual attraction to a woman what-so-ever. Which is very few since even most gay men can still find a certain woman attractive in some circumstances. If the smallest of an inkling is there, it will be amplified a hundred fold if she wishes. But on this day, she opts to teach a lesson to one of the beaches' many talented, yet conceited basketball players. Her victim today is Max, or Maxumm to be exact.

Max is 6'5", 240 pounds of well-defined, toned, brown-skinned, fine-as-hell, black man. And he knows it. If he ever had any doubt, the crowd of women that gather just to see him play, will be glad to reassure him with every ounce of their bodies, that he is *the* man. Assante remembers him well. She has to give him credit, to a degree; his dreams have a touch of eloquence. He requires her to be a different woman on every experience, many times requiring her to be 4 or 5 women at once. He has the normal staples of a dominant male dreamer. He dreams of controlling the size of his dick, making it longer and fatter as the sessions grow; you know, to get that extra scream out of her, here and there, but usually, he stays pretty close to what his true size and dimensions are, that sort of tickles her, as if he couldn't even dream himself to be better than what he truly is. But his dreams are ones of flight and fantasy. Dreams of sex in mid-flight. Dreaming often of coming to the courts, holding a woman's hand, jumping into the air, taking her with him as they float, effortlessly, and the woman is just in awe of the raw power he has. He always starts by making love to her in mid-air, floating. The more caressing and loving he is, the more tranquil the levitation is. She really likes that part. But then, the fucking starts. The pounding gets more rough, there is no affection, she is just a vessel, then they start to fall. Faster and faster, as the sex get rougher and rougher. Her screams and cries are soon drowned out by the deafening sound of the air growling into their ears. Until, when almost at terminal velocity, he cums, right before impact, and he grabs the basketball rim and yells out with a animalistic roar!!! She is his ultimate slam dunk! But he never even pays attention to her broken, shattered body on the ground. A victim of his needs, he just hangs on the rim, receiving all the applause from the crowd. He has no respect for women. He uses them, and throws them away, the dog of all dogs. Never even thinks twice. In her dream today, she will change him forever.

Assante strolls to the courts, giving small smiles and glances to all that are staring at her. But she stays on course for her primary target. Max is always at the courts early in the morning. He wants to make sure he is warmed up when all the people get there. It's 7 am, and Assante is the only woman there to watch him warm up. He sees her and stops, startled to a degree. He has that look of *"I-know-her-but-I-cant-remember-where-from,"* because he sees her as one of the reoccurring women in his dreams: a tall woman, about 5'11", slender, but with gorgeous muscular legs. She has Egyptian-style eyes, beautiful, flawless brown skin and long jet black hair. She reads his thoughts to see what his yearnings are this morning and sees the graphic image of him and her alone, late at night, having sex on this very court. So began his normal routine of showing off. His athletic ability is second to none. Jumping with ease from the free-throw line to the rim. Staying afloat for what seems an eternity with extreme grace, and unleashing tremendous power on the rim as he slams the ball through. She just stands there and smiles at him, never saying a word as he continues his display. The fact that she is not reacting with the usual "oohs and aahs" is starting to get to him. So he tries harder and harder. Now he's straining, performing feats of difficulty just to try to get some sort of reaction out of her. She sees him straining, so she lets him off the hook; she wants him uninjured for what she has planned.

"Can I try? " she says.

"Can you try what? Oh, I get it, you wanna get your dunk on?", he says, laughing and throwing her the ball. Assante dribbles the ball a little bit, but walks way out to the outer perimeter of the court, behind the 3-point line.

"You know what? Your dunks do look very pretty," she says as she lets go with an effortless jump shot, and it goes straight through the rim, snapping the net back, "but they're still only worth 2 points." This is a clear challenge to him, a statement that he would lose in a game with her. But of course this is an incredible turn-on to him, a woman with "Game".

"Is that right? I see, you got a little game on you, huh? So, you wanna play a little one-on-one? Winner buys breakfast?" There's his classic no-lose situation. If she accepts, win or lose, he has a date, and it would no doubt end up being an all-day event with her watching him play some; a nice day at the beach; and then, the sex at night on the court. But she didn't have to wait that long, she works the night shift of all night shifts. So she takes the offensive, a position she knows will make her irresistible to him. "Well, why don't we say this, winner takes all. That means, all the winner wants, anything and everything within sight. You see something you want if you win, I see something I want if I win."

"You sure you ready for that? Girl, you don't know who you're dealing with! You betta ask somebody 'bout me before you go shootin' your mouth off like that, baby. I mean, I saw *Waiting to Exhale,* too, and I'm all for women taking control of their lives and all, but you bitin' off a little more than you can chew right about now."

"You gonna play or talk? Since you're the big strong man, can I take the ball out first?" "You're serious, huh?" he laughs, "ok, take it out, I ain't got nothing to lose." Assante just smiles and says, "except the game," and she walks to the top of the court. Of course what Max doesn't know is that Assante can't miss. Nothing is beyond her ability, she is not really of this world and still has her dreamscape abilities. "We're going by 1's to 7. The three-point line counts as a 2 pointer, winner takes the ball out, and no blood, no foul." Max is a little drawn back by how forward she is; but then again, he's never lost before, a woman has no chance. As soon as she takes the ball out, she blows right by him, he barely has time to get ready; she was just a flash, a blur to him. By the time he turned around to see where she went, he was just in time to watch the first point drop.

"Dayum girl, you're fast, huh?"

" I ran a lil' track." She smiles, and takes the ball out again. This time, she only takes one step in, and launches a shot all the way across the court, 30 feet, nothing but net. All that followed was a series of the same. She made sure that he never got to touch the ball, not that it would have made any difference. She wanted to humble him in the extreme. With 6 points in the bag, it was game point. Max was sweating up a storm, and very nervous. He had never in his life been beaten so bad, and by a woman, no doubt, a woman who was laughing, and never broke a sweat.

"This is it, baby, you ready to pay up? Game point right here, boy."

"It ain't over girl, just come on!"

Oh, ok, he wants to get cocky now. Hmmm, lets see, what's the best way to end this game? He has to be at his most humble for what she has planned. Oh, now she knows! She takes the ball out, and he is on her. He really only took her seriously for the last 2 points, he knew she could hit a shot from anywhere on the court at anytime. So he was guarding her with every ounce of energy he had left. She just looked at him, smiled a little grin, she even blew him a small kiss, then took him to the hole! A fake to the left, a move to blow past him on the right, and it was all over; he fell down trying to stay with her, but she was gone! As he looked up to see the last shot fall, she stopped at the front of the rim, not shooting her last shot.

"Don't miss!" he said as he jumped up to get to her.

"I won't." she said as she jumped straight up, a 4-foot vertical leap, and rocked the rim as she dunked the last bucket. "My father always wanted a boy", she said, as he stood there amazed. He just walked to the pole and sat down, tired, exhausted, and contemplating his loss.

"You didn't even break a sweat girl, this just ain't right, dayum, I can't believe this!"

"Don't worry baby, you lost the bet, and winner takes all, so I want you to take me back to your place, now, fix me some breakfast. Then see if you can make me break out into a sweat, all over your house!"

Max thought about his situation. He was still gonna come out a winner, or so he thought. He figures that this girl may have game, and for some reason, he lost, but as far as sex goes, he knows he can handle his. Plus he doesn't have to pay for dinner; just straight sex. All he has to do is fix breakfast! Definitely a winning situation. Max has an apartment right off of the beach, right on the boardwalk. So they were 5 minutes away from being alone in his bedroom. When they arrived at his apartment, Assante looked around, seeing what would be available for the sexual activities. She looked at the kitchen table. *How tall is it? Is it sturdy enough to support her and his weight? Is it high enough for him to have a straight shot into her pussy if she lies on it, or is it gonna be too low and make him have to bend his knees, messing up his stroke?* Assante glides by the table, a little higher than waist high to her, just the right height for him.

"What do you want for breakfast, Mrs. Jordan?" This was obviously a crack at her prowess on the court. So she had forgotten that he was supposed to be making her breakfast. Because after all, she doesn't need to eat.

"Just throw together something light. You know what? Just some fruit would be fine." "That's all you want? Fruit? Ok, you won, whatever you want. Let's see, I got oranges, apples, and some watermelon. Is that ok with you?"

"It's fine," she said, and off she went to look over the rest of the apartment to see the possibilities. She went into the bathroom, and saw that the shower rod is permanently installed. *That's good, I can use that to hold on to. Oh great, a desk in the bedroom, that could be of great use! What else? What's in this small room in the back? Oh no he doesn't! He has a home gym!* It's really on now. She smiles in her excitement, putting together the order of sexual events in her mind, feeling sorry for him, but also feeling anxious for herself.

"Hey girl, whatcha gettin' into over there?" Max is coming for her with a plate of fruit in his hands. "Here you go, to the winner goes the spoils." Assante takes the plate of fruit from Max, and with a confident and sturdy manner tells him, "I won the game, so we gonna do this my way! I'm not really all that hungry for food right now. I'm hungry for satisfaction. Let's see, I've got 3 fruits on this plate; slices of oranges, apples, and watermelon. I want you to eat them, and eat me. I want you to use each fruit to make a meal out of my body. Starting with my toes, the very same toes that stomped your sorry ass on the court. Put a slice of apple in between each toe, then lick and suck 'em. I mean I want my feet to smell like a damn apple tree when you're done! Second, I want you to take the oranges and squeeze the juice all over my breasts. I want the juice to run from these perfect fuckin' tits, down my body,

to my navel, and that's gonna be your navel orange! Then start from my navel and work your way up! And you better take your time. I want my nipples to be raw from your tongue! If I ain't satisfied with anything that goes on today, I'mma show up every day in the middle of the afternoon, and wipe the court with your sorry ass in front of everyone. You won't be able to show your face around here again. And considering you live on the boardwalk, that can't be too appealing a thought to you. And last, the watermelon. You know where that goes. I want that sweet fruit all over my sweet-ass pussy! Squeeze the juice all over that pussy baby, smear it all over my clit, and put some pieces inside of me. Yo' ass is going fishin' for fruit with your tongue! When you're eating me out, and I tell you that you found my spot, you better do whatever you have to do to make sure yo' ass don't move from that spot! You understand what I'm sayun to you? You're gonna please me until I tell you to stop. And when I cum, and listen to this very good, cause your reputation depends on this. When I cum in your mouth, I want you to take it all in your mouth, every last precious drop, but don't swallow! I want you to slide up my body, look me dead in my eyes, and then swallow my cum so I can see you. I want to see you take me into your body, into your blood. I'm gonna be in your system from this day forward. Then, and only then, will I let you fuck me. And you're gonna fuck me the way I wanna be fucked! You got all that? I mean, by all means, if there is any confusion, speak now, cause once we get started, there ain't gonna be any excuses." Max just sat there on his couch, listening to what this gorgeous woman was commanding him to do, thinking to himself that he really had no choice. She had beat him so effortlessly she could surely do it again.

And this is where he lived, he was very well known. To lose the way Assante could beat him, in front of everybody, would destroy his entire reputation, and his ego. So he had no option but to do as she said, to do all she has said.

"Ok, winner takes all, you win, where do I start?" Max is more humble now than he can ever remember being in his whole life. His head is lowered, and he is standing in front of Assante.

"Strip!" Assante commands. "Strip for me! You must approach me naked, I hate it when clothing rubs against my body. It's irritating, and you wouldn't want me irritated, would you? I didn't think so. So take it off, boy, whatcha waitin' for?" Max does as she commands. He places the fruit down on the table by the couch, and starts to take his clothes off. He reaches for his shoes first. "Wait!" Assante barks. "I want you to take the shoes off last. Work around the shoes. You got shorts on, it's not gonna be a problem." Not understanding her motives, but not willing to risk questioning her at this moment, he does as she says. He has on a Chicago Bulls basketball jersey, and matching shorts. He starts now with the top. He pulls the jersey off, revealing his muscular, tall frame: his brown skin, rock-hard abs, and extremely well-defined six-pack. The center crease from his abs blends straight up into his chest. It's as though you can spill a drop of water from the cleavage in his strong, perfect chest, and it would roll all the way down that canyon of muscle, through his abs, straight to his dick! This man was bad! "Let's see the rest now, come on!" Max reaches for his shorts, slides them down, and pulls them off from around his shoes. He stands there for a moment in his black Calvin Klein briefs, the bulge of his dick very

apparent. His long legs weren't skinny as most basketball players are. His legs were very well defined and toned. Nice big calves, thick, rippling thighs. "Ok, quit being shy, man, let's see what you got!" He takes off his underwear, and again, pulls them over his shoes. There he stood, naked, except for his shoes. She wanted to see him as she imagined a naked basketball player would look. Tall, fine, but still a basketball player, because of the shoes. Assante looked at his nude body, smiling, and focused in on his dick to see if he would get shy. He didn't. Max was 7 inches limp. He could handle his own, and would never be ashamed of what he had to offer. And with that in thought, he started feeling a bit more confident. She could hear him thinking *Ok, she talked all that shit, now she sees she can't handle this dick. She's gonna change her tune soon enough when I'm wearin' her ass out.* Assante couldn't have him thinking that way. She couldn't have him feel that much in control. Max even summoned the courage to ask her why she had him keep on his shoes.

"Ok, what's the deal with the shoes, girl? Why I gotta keep on my shoes? You got a shoe fetish?" This was Assante's chance to throw him off center again, shake his confidence.

"Well, when we played, I stripped you of all your game and pride on the court, while you were in those shoes. I wanted you to strip yourself of all you had left, your clothes, while you were in those same shoes. And you did it! Cause you had to. Now don't ask me no other questions from now on. Just do as I say, and don't worry about the Why's. You gotta do it all anyway, so the Why's don't matter." Now Max was feeling as he should, helpless, as she planned. "Now come over here and undress me. But don't feel on me. You can't touch my skin until I tell you to. And your dick better not get hard while you do it either. This is all for me, it's not for your enjoyment. Now, start with my shoes. But don't bend down. Get down on your knees when you serve me!" This was sure to rob him of any dominant instincts he had left. He was to serve her on his knees. To undress her from head to toe, the exact way she was to tell him to, because he lost to her in his game. He was thinking that he was beaten on every field of play he could imagine. On the courts first, now in his own house, and it was just starting. He couldn't even be a man, he had to keep his dick from getting hard. She was controlling every aspect of the situation. And there was nothing he could do about it.

Assante reads his thoughts and feels extreme gratification in his humbleness. She stands there in front of him, with him on his knees, and sticks one foot out. Max just keeps his head down never looking into her eyes, like a submissive animal, and unties her shoes, one at a time. Then he removes her socks. " Now, unbraid my hair before you take off my shirt." In the form Assante has assumed, she has long black hair that hangs half way down her back, and it's styled in a french braid. " You may stand up for this part." Max does as she says. She doesn't even turn around so he can unbraid her hair, she makes him walk around the table to get behind her. Max unbraids her hair, being especially careful not to touch her back with his hands. She told him not to touch her. Occasionally, Assante peeks into his mind to see what he is thinking. Currently, all he can concentrate on is doing everything right so she won't get mad. She is loving it; *this is what dreams are made of!* When he's done with her hair, she says, "Now the shirt! But fold it right after you take it off. Don't get any of my clothes wrinkled! I don't want my appearance after I'm done here to reflect what I'm going to do to you." Max concentrates as hard as he can, being extremely careful to lift her shirt without wrinkling it, or touching her. Then he lays her shirt down carefully on top of his stereo. He looks at Assante. How perfect she is, her hair flowing down her back like an ocean of black waves. She has on a black bra, half lace, half translucent silk. He can see her nipples clear as day through the silk fabric. Then he feels his dick getting hard. He can't help it, she is so gorgeous, the sexiest woman he has ever seen! Assante doesn't need to use her mind-reading ability to notice that he is getting hard. "If your dick gets hard, your life is gonna get a whole lot harder! Think about that and get your horny ass under control! For once in your life you're not gonna think about yourself, but instead you'll only think of the needs of a woman! Now take off my bra, my breasts need to breathe!" The bra unhooks in the front. This is torture to Max. But for the first time he thinks what Assante wants him to think. For the first time he is thinking that he can't wait to serve her. He is only thinking about licking her body, and eating her out. He is not thinking of his own gratification. And Assante finally starts to get wet. She wants to know exactly how he is feeling right now, but her ability to actually share the physical feelings of others only comes while they are in physical contact with her, that's why she told him not to touch her. She wants something to look forward to.

Max unhooks the bra, and sees Assante's 40C chest standing at attention, as if the bra was still holding her breasts up. He is amazed at how this woman is more than he could have dreamed, not knowing that she is exactly what he has dreamed. "You're doing better, good boy, now slide my shorts down, but remember, don't get 'em all wrinkled. And get back on your knees!" As Max drops down to his knees and slides her shorts down, he can see the ripples in her thighs. He thinks of having those thighs wrapped around his head while he is giving her the pleasure she has demanded. Assante reads his mind and knows that he is almost ready to serve her. She has almost broken his urge to destroy a woman, and changed it into a yearning to serve. She gets very wet. Max can smell Assante's wetness. Assante releases pure pheromones, after all, she is literally a pure sexual being. Assante knows that by the time Max takes her panties off, all he will want to do is serve her. He'll be begging her for the honor of licking her body soon. Max is there, on his floor, on bended knee, looking at the matching black lace and translucent silk panties Assante has on. Her lips are open, her panties are wet, and he almost wants to cry because he is using all his will to not get hard. It's not possible! The pheromones are driving him crazy, he doesn't know what is happening to him. All he knows is that he has to please this woman. Assante is about to really give him hell for getting hard until she reads his mind, because all she sees are visions of him eating her out. The only thoughts he has is of her in ultimate pleasure. So she lets him have his rock-hard erection, only because what is making him hard is the thought of her being pleased. Now he is ready to serve, and Assante is ready to feel what he feels; she's ready to feed off of him.

Assante lays down on the couch. She chooses the couch because she knows that when it comes time for him to eat her out, he can stay on his knees, on the floor, and get to her really good on the couch. She lays back, and simply points to the apples on the plate. With her only gesture being a raised eyebrow, and a foot slid out in front of his face, she has ordered him to start. Max takes to his mission of servitude willingly. He gently caresses her foot, his body relaxes and his eyes close for a moment -- he treasures even this little moment of finally touching her feet -- and takes four slices of apple. He slides them in between each of her toes, and looks up at her for a signal that he's done right. She gives a little grin, saying, "take another piece and paint my entire foot with it, lick my foot clean, then go for the other slices." He obeys without hesitation. He takes a fifth piece and starts to rub her foot with the apple slice, over the top of her feet, down to the back of her foot, under the sensitive, tender sole. It tickles, she wants to squirm, but she has to stay strong too. The whole time he touches her, he holds her foot as if she is made of glass; he is in awe of her. Again, when he is done covering her foot with the apple, he glances up for approval, he gets the nod, and he starts to lick her feet clean. This is the first time Max's tongue touches her body, right in the middle of her sole, and the mere contact of her flesh on his tongue makes his dick jump up and slap him right in the middle of his stomach. Now that he is touching her, Assante can finally experience all of him, she can tap into what his body is feeling; it's a real rush! She feels the muscles in his dick straining so hard, it makes his dick sore! She also feels the effect the pheromones are having on his system, making him light headed, literally drunk with the essence of sex. Assante lays there, feeling him lick her, she knows this is the start to a long session, and she starts to relax and enjoy it. Max first licks her up and down in long licks across the sole of her feet, then in small circles. He really gets into his job, she gives him that. He does the same across the top of her foot, then the ball of her foot. He finally makes his way to the slices in between her toes. He caresses her foot and kisses each toe, softly as if they would break if he pressed on them too hard. Then he starts at the first apple, the one in between her big toe and her second toe. He nibbles at the corners of the slice, chewing them down from the front and the back until there is only a small piece left in between. He takes his fingers, gently splits her toes, then, tips the remaining piece into his mouth with the tip of his tongue. While he still has her toes open, he slides his tongue up and down the " v-shaped " crevice, assimilating the way he is gonna eat her out later. Slowly and carefully, he repeats the process until both feet have been thoroughly cleansed and consumed. Looking up once again to make sure this first phase was satisfactorily completed, he gets a simple acknowledgment of her single index finger, coaxing him upward.

Step two of his mission, her breasts. She was laying down on the couch, totally relaxed. The room now smelled of fruit and sex. The smell was so thick in Max's mind that he could taste the very air he was breathing. Max was totally in tune with her body now, he had never given a woman this much thought before, and now, all he could think about was her body, and her pleasure. As he crawled up the couch, sliding past her legs, on the way up to her navel, he passes her pussy and the pure pheromones hit him, making his head spin and all his nerves tingle. He is so into the experience, he is concentrating so hard on her needs, his senses seem to be much more acute. As he kneels there next to her body, his face a centime-

ter away from touching her navel, he can feel the heat rising up from her body. Again Assante reads his mind and now since he is not touching her, she can't feel him. In his mind, he sees her stomach like hot sand with heat waves rising up to strangle him. Her body is a flawless desert of brown sand, and he imagines that his tongue will be scorched if he doesn't cool her down. The only thing that will cool her hot body , is the cool oranges. He reaches for the orange slices and turns to hold them over Assante's breasts. He glances down at her to make sure he can proceed, and Assante just closes her eyes and arches her back to raise her breasts higher, near his hands. The juice must roll down her body. Then he squeezes the oranges right onto her nipples. Her body was hot, and the cold orange juice almost stung her as she felt her nipples tighten and come alive in their firmness. Max grabbed 3 slices in each hand and squeezed the juice again, all over her breasts, and watched the orange, flowing ocean run down the middle of her hot, brown desert. He looked at his hands, the juice dripping off of them in slow motion, squeezing the slices harder to cover her body, to add to the ocean, the juice swirling cold in between his fingers, dripping down to join the river now forming on Assante's hot, perfect body. His sandy desert now had a orange oasis to cool his tongue in, and in that oasis is where he was to start. He looked at her navel for a moment, saw how each breath she took made the orange pool rock back and forth. He approached her slowly, easing his way to her navel, and then, he held his breath as he went down to lick her. He saw her body as a perfect picture, the still pool as a perfect mirror, he didn't want his breath to cause a single ripple. Slowly, he parted his lips and let his tongue enter the pool. Straight down,

like a diver entering the water. He didn't suck up the juice, he just put his tongue in and stirred it around. Contact! That's what Assante was waiting for; immediately she wanted to add the sensations he was feeling to her own, to feel double the pleasure. As she felt the cold liquid run down her body, and the air in the room blowing against the juices now covering her, she could feel the sensations on his tongue, exactly as if her tongue was now cool with the juice he was licking off her body. As he swirled his tongue around her navel, she could feel the juice on the front and back of her tongue, not to mention the feeling she was getting directly, the deep licking he was giving her. He finally lowers his lips into the pool and sucks her navel dry, slowly swirling his tongue around her navel the whole time. "Now, suck my tits baby, work your way up." He was now on his way up to her breasts. Just as he did with her toes, he was taking long licks up her torso, following with circles. He could smell her skin and the juice mixing together. He couldn't wait to have her nipples in his mouth; she couldn't wait to feel his tongue on her rock-hard nipples. When he reached her breasts, he took a long lick up her cleavage, then began his pattern of circles. She took her breasts in her hands and pressed them against the side of his head. She wanted to smother him, to consume his head in her breasts. As she held her breasts against his ears, she could feel him still licking; he was worried more about pleasing her than breathing! "My nipples! Now!" No sooner said than done. He took hold of her left breast in his big hands, and totally submerged her nipple into his mouth. While he sucked on her hard, orange-flavored nipple, he rolled it around on his tongue. He rolled her nipple slowly, round and round, then flicked his

tongue quickly, back and forth. The whole time never letting the cold air get to her nipple, the only air she felt was the hot air in his mouth. As he sucked on her left nipple, he now played with her right one. Using his right hand to tease it, she could feel the sensation of him sucking and teasing her nipples, it was as though her nipples were connected to her clit, and she could feel every lick, suck and flick go straight to her clit. "Harder!," she said, "Harder, suck me harder! And pinch, fuck, pinch me harder!" She could feel the immediate reaction to her commands. She felt more of her breast rise like magic into his mouth, the added pressure of his tongue clamping against her nipple and the extreme sucking he was giving her was making it feel like her tit was gonna turn inside out! Her right nipple was in his fingers, and he started with a slight pinch, and worked his way up to a slightly painful, but extremely pleasurable twist. "Switch!," she whispered as she was almost out of breath. And switch he did, giving the opposite breast the same treatment. "Now lick me clean." Assante wanted each part of the meal to be completed in full before the next course was to commence. Max licked every inch of her breasts, even her neck, then back down to her navel to her trimmed pubic hairs, and followed the trim triangle to her pussy, then stopped, not actually licking her until the watermelon was applied.

Once again, he glanced up to make sure he can proceed. The only signal this time was how Assante was starting to reposition herself. With Max still on his knees, she sat facing him, her back against the cushion, leaning with her legs open, so her pussy was slightly out past the seat cushions. He had nothing to get in his way from doing what he had to do, and he couldn't wait. He reached over again, to get the last of the fruit from the tray, the watermelon. The watermelon was seedless and cut into small cubes, and was still very cool. Assante leaned back, closed her eyes, rested her hands on the top of her thighs and said, "Ummm, now, finish your breakfast, and don't forget to put some inside me, so you can go fishin." Assante was ready to cum already. The anticipation of him licking her clit the way he licked her nipples was driving her crazy. But she had to stay cool, she dare not let him see her sweat, although she truly already was. As he picked the watermelon up from the plate, she got extremely excited just to see him place them in his hands and get ready to squeeze, anticipating the cool, sticky juice. Max held his hands right over her pussy. One actually over her clit, the other, over her hole, then squeezed! The cold drops made her jump a little at first, but the juice mixed in quickly with her own juices, and melted all over her pussy. Assante wanted to cum off of his first lick, after all the anticipation and foreplay, she was ready, and his first lick was a good one. A long, hot, forceful lick, like a wet dick sliding from her hole to her clit. His goatee was tickling her like it was pubic hairs. Assante knew what was next, he had a pattern that he followed, first the long lick, then, the slow circles, from hole to clit, over and over; lick, then the circles. "Ummm, yeah...lick that pussy baby," Assante said. Max was fondling each and every one of her lips along the way. He licked her for about 30 minutes that way. Then Assante said "time to go fishin'." With that being said, Max grabbed another piece of watermelon, and bit it in half and placed one half on the plate while he kept the other half in his hand. He wiped his mouth a bit first, getting her wetness from his chin, and licked it off his fingers. Then he slowly put the cold piece of watermelon inside of her. The piece was small, so it went in smooth. It was cold at first, making her muscles constrict around it until it warmed up and she could relax again. Then Max went after it! He didn't go at her soft this time, he knew she was way past the slow and easy stage. He stuck his tongue deep into her pussy, forceful and fast! He went fishin' for that watermelon alright, his tongue was bouncing around in her pussy like she was getting eaten out by a blender! She couldn't take it, she was gonna cum. It had been building up for hours now, and now he was tongue fucking her, in and out, round and round, he wasn't gonna stop until she told him to, and she couldn't even talk at the moment so he was never gonna stop! She looked down and saw that fine-ass face in between her legs, and she came right when he got the watermelon! "Ohhhh, hell yeah!!!!! Oh, shit, oh shit!!!! Suck me!!! Fuckin' take me all in your mouth!!!!!" She came so hard, that while his tongue was retrieving the watermelon, his mouth filled with her cum. But he remembered what she told him, not to swallow, that is, not until she could see him swallow. When she was done, she grabbed him by the back of his bald head and eased him up to her face. They locked stares, and while looking right into her eyes, he swallowed her. She watched as he took her into his body, and she got incredibly turned on again. She wanted more! " Now the clit," she said, pointing at the half piece of watermelon on the plate. He knew what she wanted. So again, he dropped down to serve her. He took the half piece of cool fruit, and smeared it directly onto her clit. Her clit was swollen and extremely sensitive, the feeling was orgasmic and agonizing at the same time, but the best was yet to come. Before she could think to say it, Max had her clit in his mouth. Just like he did with her nipples, he was rolling her smooth clit around in circles with his tongue. Then came the fast licks, up and down, faster and faster, damn, she was ready to cum again! "That's it! Don't move...ohh, shit!!!!!! Here I cum!!!" Once again, she came all over his face; he was on her clit and not inside her as before, so it got all over his neck. Assante, still in the middle of her orgasm wanted to top it off, so, while he was still massaging her clit in his mouth, she did a physical tap. She wanted to know what he felt, and it was unbelievable. She could feel her own smooth, tender clit on the tip of her tongue. As he licked and teased her clit, she could feel it bouncing around on her tongue, she could even taste the watermelon in her mouth. This was the ultimate. She went into orgasmic seizures, one after another, feeling her pussy jump in her mouth, filling up his mouth, as well as feeling her own violent orgasms. She finally had to pull his head off of her because she couldn't cum anymore; it was actually hurting. Out of breath, and weak from losing count of how many times she came, she looked at Max, and he was very pleased with himself. Her conquest was almost complete. His lesson almost learned. All that remained was the fucking, and then his final punishment for the years he had used her.

Max had been completely quiet up to this point. All he did was follow commands; up until now he had no reason for words. "I'm finished with breakfast." That's all he said. A small smile on his face, and still on his knees, wiping his chin and his neck off, licking his hands and fingers again, swallowing all he could of this dream woman. With his head still cloudy from the raw pheromones he had just inhaled and

digested for the last hour he had been eating Assante out, she doesn't give him, or herself time to rest. "Now, fuck me! Like I said, you're gonna fuck me the way I wanna be fucked. If yo' ass is the type that cums quick, you betta do what you gotta do to control it. Think of basketball or whatever you gotta do, but you betta not cum till I give your permission! Now carry me to the table, lay me on top, and fuck the hell outta my ass!" Max, when fully erect, is a strong, thick, 10 and ½ inches. Normally, the only thought that goes through his mind before sex is what part of her body is he gonna cum on. Is he gonna cum on her ass, maybe her back, her tits, her neck, or his favorite, her face!? Max was like that, the more he degraded a woman, the more he got turned on. But for the first time in his selfish life, he was giving, and someone had come on his face. He knew in his mind that he was a man, and he was about to get him some. But he still felt like although he was the one with the dick, he was the one that was going to get fucked, and Assante was going to do the fucking! Max picks Assante up with ease, in her current form she only weighs 135 pounds, no problem for a man of his build to handle, and he lays her down on the kitchen table. "Fuck me! I said Fuck me, boy! You betta wear this pussy out so I'm too tired to wear yo' tired ass out on that court!" Max looks at Assante lying on the table, naked, legs spread open, and waiting for him, and he gets a surge of energy. All of a sudden he feels like he's *the man* again! Big mistake on his part, but he doesn't know that. Assante measures Max up really quick. Thinking to herself, *Hmmm...let's see, 10 ½ inches, ok, he's used ta hittin bottom real quick. Let's see....* Assante changes the depth of her pussy to be just out of Max's reach. She continues to think. *Pretty thick too, he's surely used ta rippin' walls up..no problem...* She adjusts her width with but a thought. As she finishes her preparations, Max is in her. He is surprised as hell when she doesn't scream from his sudden entry. She just takes his long, fat dick in stride. "I said fuck me!" With that being said, Max digs down to handle the task. Max is used to competition, and he'd never lost in the sport of fucking before. Making love, he's never been good at, but fucking, now he always had that under control. But now this woman was turning him out! *Hell no,* he thought. *Ain't no way I'm goin' out like this, I got a fine-ass woman up in here like this, on my table, and she gonna get the best of me? She ain't knowin!* Max looks at her, laying there, fine as hell, bucking back and forth on his dick, literally fucking him, and he gets more excited, growing another ½ inch inside of her and hitting her back wall. She didn't give herself enough room, and she yells out, "Ohh shit!!!!" She was caught off guard, and knows that Max has just got a tremendous ego boost cause now he's going at her like his life depends on it. Damn, what does she do now, she just can't change her dimensions again, that's not natural, she knew better. She made a mistake in calculating his size, and now she had to take it. Damn it, just like in her reality, in his dreams, he was fucking her, making her scream, and she knew he was gonna try to wear her ass out, she got him more ready then he's ever been before, this was gonna be a fucking of a lifetime for him, and almost like another day at work for her.. She tried to hold it back, but she couldn't help it, he got bigger, and she couldn't get any deeper. She'd made a grave mistake. She was used to men growing more in their dreams, but with all the excitement, she was not prepared for Max to grow in reality. It's as though he wanted her so bad, his ego was trampled so thoroughly, the human side of him, the side of him that made him a man, literally willed himself bigger. Now she had to contend with her situation. She didn't know how true human females could deal with this man, how did they handle him? With every stroke, Max got more and more forceful. Soon it got so bad she could barely breathe. She tried to squirm back a bit, but Max was too strong for her. He just picked her up by her waist and pulled her towards him, lifting her ass off the table and throwing her onto his dick while he thrust to fill her up. She was filled to capacity, and he had her locked onto his dick, wearing her long legs like a belt around his waist. In this position she was too vulnerable, she had to gain the upper hand, she had to regain control . She thought about using her gifts, to make herself stronger than he was, an easy enough task, but then she pondered her situation. It was more fun this way, she had to think, she had to be resourceful. She was actually laughing at herself for getting in this situation. With that being decided, she knew she had to fuck him back, she had to take it. With her legs still wrapped around his waist, she raised up to grab his arms which were locked on her waist, and she pulled herself up. While he was inside of her, she strained, scratching up from his forearms, to his elbows, past his biceps, to his shoulders. When she got to his shoulders she took a deep breath. She was going to wrap her arms around the back of his neck and hold on, making him fuck her standing up, but he was still all the way deep inside of her, and she knew the angle change was gonna hurt her. She gritted her teeth and made the final move, and when she did, Max grabbed her ass and started bouncing her on his dick! Max had no intentions of ever letting up, but she knew this position would tire him out faster, because he had to support both their weights and absorb all the shock of him bouncing her on him. She was in pain, but she was excited. Now she understood what "It-hurt-in-a-good-way" meant. She grabbed the back of his head and kissed him hard, but it was a short kiss because they were both breathing so hard. She was trying not to scream loud, she knew that would fuel him more, so she just bit down on his shoulder. Max was finally starting to tire, but in his determination, he wasn't going to quit. She didn't know how he was getting the energy. She thought about doing a physical tap, but stopped herself, wanting to enjoy this part as a woman, giving herself the same handicaps a normal woman would have. She knew Max would have to do something soon, he was human, and he was getting tired. She could feel his legs shaking, getting weaker, and his penetration had gotten more shallow. She thought about the desk in the bedroom. He could put her there. *HELL NO!* That would put her right back in the position she was getting out of in the kitchen. Then she remembered the gym in the back room. That was the next location.

"Strap me up in those fuckin' cables in the back! This is gonna be the best workout you eva had!" No sooner said than done. Max didn't say a word, he just started to walk them both to the back room, still, her legs around his waist, fucking her the whole way. When they got to the back room, she quickly surveyed the home gym set once again. A full array of cables with arm and leg straps. "Lay down on the bench, I wanna ride your fuckin' ass." Finally Max pulls out and she feels 10 pounds lighter without him inside of her. Max lays down on the bench, his back against the board like he was about to work the fuck out, and he was about to work it out on her. The sweat on his body was dripping, the only light was coming through a small window on the opposite side of the room, and the light was hitting him just right to really show off every rippling, straining, tight muscle. Not to mention how his dick looked, poised there, waiting for her to mount him. As he laid there, Assante took the offensive again, she saw that there were 4 straps on the gym set. 2 for the legs, 2 for the arms. She tied his legs and arms into the straps, and set the weights to their highest level so he couldn't move. There he lay, strapped down, his knees bent at the end of the bench, with his feet flat on the floor. His arms were hanging straight down off the bench, he could grab the carpet in his hands. He was helpless again, and she was getting her second wind! Assante was tall enough to stand over him while he lay in between her legs on the bench. The bench was about knee high to her so she could ride him standing up, just bending her knees to bounce up and down. She just stood there for a while, she had to really admire his body, it was as if he were a creature of the dreamscape, he was physically as flawless as she. She stood over him and clawed her nails into his chest. His pecs flexed as she scratched him all the way down his torso, slowly feeling the muscles and the definition in her palms. She loved the way her fingers fell into the crevices in his six pack, she loved to just watch him breathe, to watch his chest move up and down. She couldn't wait any longer, she had to have him inside, she had to feel raw muscle deep inside her body while she rode this pure mass of power. She stood in front of his dick, and reached back with one hand to grab it off his stomach, and held it straight up so she could mount him. Damn, she had to get on

her tiptoes just to get on top of it! Then she lowered herself slowly onto him. With about 4 inches of himself inside of her, he arched his back and thrust his dick all the way into her. "Ohhhhh Shit!!!!!" Assante growled, sucking the air hard in between her gritted teeth. She put her hands down on his chest to catch her balance while she tried to raise her body higher than her tiptoes can get her. She thinks about the situation. *That shit hurt! Maybe this wasn't a good idea after all. Fuck that, I'mma beat his ass. I can handle this shit; if he's gonna learn, I gotta do this right. I can't fail now, it'll only make him worse, and ruin all I'm tryun to accomplish.* She knew she had to break Max, she had to ride him, and break him just like he was a bull. She put one hand on his chest, and put the other hand around this throat and leaned down in his face. "You think you gonna fuck me like dat? Nigga, I'mma fuck you 'til you think your mutha fuckin' dick is gonna break off! Let's see how yo' punk ass can handle that shit!" Assante then remounts him, this time forcefully. She looks him dead in the eyes as she drops all the way down on him. It's an exercise in discipline, she doesn't even blink as she takes all 11 inches of his rock-hard dick into her. You can hear the slapping of skin as she literally jumps up and down on him, riding him viciously, dropping down to grind in long, full circles. Breathing heavily, she says, "Huh, what, you say? You awfully quiet! Fuck me like a man, nigga, what's wrong? Come on, you used ta tell women to take that dick, huh! Well take this pussy, nigga! Take this mutha fuckin' pussy!" Assante is in a zone, she is trying to break Max back down. Max is in a helpless position, strapped down. He wants to grab her around her waist and bounce her on his dick so bad, he wants control right now, but there's nothing he can do. She is leaning over him now, her hair falling in his face. He keeps trying to lift his head to kiss her, but she keeps pulling back, just out of his reach, teasing him. He has to do something, anything at all. She is fucking the shit out of him and he can't even touch her. With all the strength he can muster, he flexes his arms up to grab the back of her head. Each arm must have 150 pounds strapped to it, but he has to kiss her lips, he has to touch that hair. Assante sees his biceps turn into straining, round, hard rocks, veins carrying blood to the yearning arms. She can't believe what she is seeing. What is driving him so hard, why is he so determined? She has to know if it is physical, she has to do a physical tap. She taps into Max and the rush of feelings almost takes over her; it makes her stop riding for a second. It's a lot to handle. She can feel what it feels like to have a long, strong dick inside a woman. She can feel how the muscles in his arms are burning, but still rising up towards her, winning the battle against the weight that binds them. She is lost in a sea of physical ecstasy as she feels as though she is fucking herself, feeling the man inside of her, but also feeling the woman on top of him. Then she is startled as she feels what seems to be hair in her hands, but they're not her hands, they're really his. He won his battle, he has her hair and with a sudden yank of her hair, her concentration is broken, and the tap is gone. He has her now, and with his arms straining to stay up, the relentless weights forever working against him, he pulls her down for the kiss. She starts to ride him again as he kisses her hard, knowing it is hurting him just to make the effort, his tongue pressing hard against hers, his eyes closed hard, concentrating on keeping the weight up, then his arms fail him, and the battle

with the weights is over. His arms fall back down, and he has expended most of his energy. For a moment she rides him more softly; she is actually touched by his effort to reach her, the amount of sacrifice he made just to kiss her lips. She feels her heart fill, as she is overcome with emotion, she is also overcome with the incredible turn on of this man's strength and determination. His raw power inside of her, filling her up, building up another orgasm, she tried to slow her stroke down, she had cum so many times earlier, she was now sore, and another orgasm would hurt, but Max feels her walls shaking and knows she is ready, and with all he has left, he rises up into her, bucking into her, and she cums. She digs into his chest, and he sees a tear fall from her eye. She is spent, she has no energy left. She dismounts him, and decides to give him the opportunity to be *the man*. The effort he has put forth to this point, has slowly eroded away her memories of all the years he has used her in his dreams. She quickly unstraps him, "Get up, it's your turn, strap my legs down." She looks at him softly, she is giving herself to him. With that, he moves, and she lays down. She lays down on her stomach, and straps one of her hands in. "Come get my other hand." Max hurries and straps her legs down with the cables, then goes to strap her other arm down. Here she lay, flat on her stomach with her legs spread open, feet strapped in, and her ass out. He wastes no time in taking his turn at fucking her as she lie helpless. He stood behind her, bent his knees, and entered her surprisingly slow. He was actually gentle, and she really loved the way she was feeling, how he was making her feel. She felt herself drifting, getting lost in the moment, actually feeling sorry for how she talked to him earlier. "I'm sorry, baby," she whispered. It literally slipped out of her mouth, involuntarily. She wasn't too accustomed to real-world emotions. Then everything changed. Max seemed like he snapped out of a trance of some sort, and got extremely rough. She was strapped in, and he got a new-found energy from somewhere. He was going at her again, grinding hard in circles, she could feel her walls stretching like he was gonna tear through her, and she couldn't move. He started slapping her ass, pulling her hair back, getting rougher and rougher. "Yeah, you though you was gonna fuck me and play me like that? Fuck that, you ain't too bad now are ya, bitch! Uh huh, that's right, lay there and take this fuckin' dick, bitch!" *Oh no he didn't! Ohhhh hell no!* Assante quickly feels an extreme amount of anger rise in her body. She can no longer feel pleasure. It's like she can't even feel him inside of her anymore. She is mad at herself for losing sight of why she was there, to get payback for all the years that he used her in her reality, in his dreams. She got played; a being of limitless possibilities, and she got played. She read his mind to see what the hell he could have been thinking about, and there she saw it, the image of him pulling her hair back and cumming all over her neck, even in her ears! Now she was pissed! She pulled her arms together like the weights weren't even there. She did it so fast, Max didn't notice how she was all of a sudden free. She was on the loose again, and she had a renewed sense of purpose.

"Let's move! Come on, I want it in the shower!," said Assante.

"Go ahead and get loose, I'll get the water goin'," replied Max, and off he went to the bathroom to get the shower ready. Assante was so mad she didn't just unstrap her legs, she broke the cables in half. Cables that could suspend over 2,000 pounds in weight, just snapped as if they were kite string. Oh yeah, the kid gloves were off, he called her a bitch, pissed her off, he disrespected a sexual entity of untold of power, and now, she was on her way to get him. The way he disrespected her, the thoughts he was having, just upped the ante on his final punishment. She was going to let him off the hook with a verbal talk, telling him to respect women, and to learn to love. But now, the way he showed his ass; wait, he was gonna cum in her ears, in HER EARS!!!! No, he had to pay! This boy was about to have some serious issues.

When Assante reaches the bathroom, Max is there, testing the water, wearing a smile on his face; the water must be ready. She slides by him, and gets into the shower, wetting her whole body, coaxing him in by rubbing on her nipples. Max has a huge grin on his face as he can't wait to finish where he left off. Assante is happy to oblige him, as much easier to let someone dig their own grave than to dig it for them yourself. She was going to turn around, stick her ass out, and let him get his "dig on". That's just what she did, she turned around so she faced the shower streams, and let the water run down her face. With her hands pressed against the wall, she stood there as if a police officer were going to frisk her, but Max was the only one with a night stick here at the time. Max gets right to it, he's going at her with full gusto. She plays into his hand, plays the "you're-hurting-me" role. She knows this will send Max into a fucking frenzy, and it does. The shower is a big walk-in enclosure, more than enough room for Max to maneuver, and he has Assante by the waist, ripping into her from behind. Assante "pleaded" with him, "Please stop, fuck, it's killing me! You're tearing me apart!" This just sends Max into a rage! All you can hear is the slap of the skin, of flesh ramming against flesh! Then Assante starts to bleed. She looks down, crying, acting surprised, saying, "Oh my god, I'm bleeding! I'm bleeding! What have you done!? Oh shit, I told you, you were hurting me! Stop, STOP!!" Assante quickly steps away from Max, shuffling into the corner of the shower to survey her "damage". But Max is having none of that. He charges her, pinning her into the corner. He *knows* he's the dominant one in this situation, he *knows* he's the strongest out of the two, he *knows* he has total control over what happens, but what he doesn't *know*, is that everything he *knows*, is **wrong!** Max pins Assante in the corner of the shower. He pushes her hard against the wall with his left hand against her torso, and wraps his right hand around her neck. Assante looks at him as if she's terrified, as he leans in close, "Fuck that shit, bitch! I ain't done with you yet! You gonna take it till I'm finished, and you ain't gonna say shit about this to nobody! You got that!? If you even think about runnin yo' ass to the police and cry rape, they will laugh yo' ass out the station. The cops here are my boys; they all know me, shit, we all play ball together, so yo' ass ain't got any options here. Now quit your dayum cryun, shut the fuck up, bitch!" That was all Assante needed to hear. She was reading his mind, she knew he was thinking about raping her, that he was going to be commit the ultimate in selfish acts. She just wanted him to actually commit the rape, she wanted to make sure his punishment would fit his crime, and it did.

As Max had his hand wrapped around her neck, he goes to insert himself inside her once again, and finish the rape.

Then the look of terror leaves Assante's face as she looks up, looks him dead in his eyes, and cracks a grin. Max is taken aback by this a bit. *Why is she grinning at me, what's goin' on?* He instantly feels uneasy as he knows something isn't right. In all the other times he'd raped a woman, never once had she smiled at him for doing it. But now Assante is staring at him with a pleased look on her face; she seems very content with her situation, and she is just staring Max down. Max decides it's a mind game, and he's going to wipe that smile off her face! "Don't smile at me, bitch!," he yells, as he slaps her across her face. The sound of the slap is extremely loud against her wet skin. But Assante's head doesn't even shake with the blow, she just stands there, not blinking, grinning at him, staring him right in the eyes. Max, now feeling extremely uneasy, tries harder. "Bitch, I said don't smile at me!!!" This time he lets go with a full-fisted blow to her mouth. Again, the blow connects, but not even as much as a flinch comes from Assante, not even a blink. Now Max is scared. *How is that possible?* He hit her with everything he had! She's a woman, she should have been knocked out by that last blow. He feels his fear rising, he doesn't know how to feel exactly, but he's nervous. One of our most primal instincts tells us when we're being hunted. Assante stays clam, like the calm a snake displays just before it strikes.

Max can't take it anymore, he doesn't know what to do, he has to get some sort of reaction out of her, a yell, a scream, a tear, even a single blink would suffice! So he goes to strike her again, but this time, as he clenches his fist and reaches back, Assante retaliates. With seemingly inhuman speed, she's on him. Her hands fly up in a blur, wrap around his neck, as she

lifts him off the ground and tosses him through the air against the hard tile walls. Max doesn't even get a chance to hit the ground before he feels his ribs being crushed, blow after blow, by hands that feel like steel. He feels his insides shaking with every blow. The blows are coming so fast he has no time to react, he can't breathe, the hot, thick air is suffocating him as the rate of the punches increases. Now the blows are coming 3 or 4 per second, constant, deadly, precise, to the kidneys, ribs, and stomach. All Max can utter is a small plead while he still has some breath left in him. "Stop, please, stop." The plea is but a whisper as he can barely get air into his abused lungs and shattered rib cage. "What did you say?," Assante says and stops momentarily and leans in to hear Max beg once again. Max is now sliding to the floor, doubled over in the fetal position holding his ribs, gasping for air as the water is falling in his face, choking him. "Stop, please, I'm sorry, I'm sorry." Assante looks at him. He's crawling on the floor, trying to get out of the path of the water stream so he can breathe. As Max finally crawls closer to the door, Assante attacks again! "Fuck that shit, bitch! I ain't done with you yet! You gonna take it till I'm finished! Sound familiar, mutha fucka!!??" This time the attack is focused on his limbs. She bounces him off the walls of the shower violently. You can hear the sounds of bones snapping as his legs and arms are now flopping around with shattered bones, as tiles are falling off the shower walls, jarred loose by the ferocity of the attack! Max's whole body goes limp as Assante senses he's about to lose consciousness, so she stops, she wants him to remain conscious through the whole ordeal. There he lay, on the tile floor, the blood mixing in with the water, swirling round and round the drain, steadily flowing, an accurate gauge to the violence of the attack.

"What's wrong Shugga? Looks like you need a docta." She laughs as she crouches down next to him on the floor. He sees her coming for him again, but he doesn't even have the strength to lift his head. He just watches as she approaches, his eyes are wide with terror. Now the sounds of sirens can be heard nearby. Someone must have heard all the noise and called the police. Time was now very limited. Assante glides her hands slowly, and gently across his face, caressing his cheeks in her hand. As Max closes his eyes, relaxing, feeling the attack is finally over, Assante digs her fingernails into his skin, slowly, deeper and deeper. When blood starts flowing from his face, and down her fingers, she rakes her hands from his head, down his eyelids, across his cheeks and jaws, over to his mouth, splitting his lips, down his chin, and across his neck. His whole face is bloody, as if he were wearing a mask of blood. "Now you wear the face on the outside, of the scarred-bastard-monster you are on the inside!". As she speaks those words, she can hear the police cars screech to a halt outside. It's time for her to go. As she rises, and looks at Max's bloody, and shattered, broken body laying on the floor, she smiles as she remembers that this is the exact way she looked in his dreams after he was done with her. She sees life imitating dreams, as he lay, befittingly in the same pose as she did, on his dreamscape court, shattered bones, disfigured face, and she was walking away from him, without a care in the world. As she leaves the shower, she peeks back in with one last thought, "I GOT YOUR BITCH!!!," as she laughs, and heads for the door.

She opens the front door, steps out, and right after she closes the door, the police are on their way in. The 4 male cops

pause as they spot her, but Assante just walks right towards them, confident, not bothered by their reaction to her. For she knows they aren't looking at her as a suspect, their hesitation isn't one of warning, but one of amazement. As they each see her as a different woman, all four of he forms are different, yet gorgeous. To never be identified, a perfect alibi, and part of her unearthly creation. She continues towards them, smiles at each one, and walks by, right out the door.

As she walks down the boardwalk of the beach, she sees the sun setting, and knows it is time for her to wake up into the dreamscape, and fulfill the fantasies of the human night. But this night, she was sure that Max wouldn't be dreaming thoughts of sexual conquest, she knew that this night she would be free of the man of flight and fantasy. She finds a secluded area behind a dumpster, where she dissipates, vanishes with the evening dusk. She's gone.

As for Max, he would never walk again. Never again would he feel the freedom of gliding through the air. Never again would he experience the exhilaration of being the best on the court. Never again would he be able to look in the mirror and admire his flawless skin, for the scars on his face had turned into keloids, and he was now a disfigured shell of the man he once was.

The Daydreamers walk amongst us, were you nice to the lover in your dreams?

Wicked

First Penetration

That first penetration,
How do I define.
That one sexual moment,
That stops my heart, and blows my mind!

When I'm so fuckin' hard,
My dick is sore with throbbing veins.
That first penetration,
Is the only savior to my pain.

Like hot, thick,
Molten wax.
Dripping from my head,
Sliding down my shaft.

Liquid suffocation,
So my dick can't breathe,
Dammit PENETRATION,
PERFECT pussy, Fill my needs!!!!

Every inch,
Caressed, by those hot, soft lips.
Whew! That first penetration,
Lord, Thank You, for my woman's gift!

<u>RAW</u>

Gentle is not my true nature,
As I attack the pussy, ummm, with those lips parted.
I'm a deep-down freak, no inhibitions,
I like my shit Raw, so let's get it started!

The second yo' ass hits the door,
I'll grab your hair and drop you to the floor!
Assume the position! **Ass up, Face down!**
Time for Raw Fuckin'! Ain't no time ta clown!

I'll consume your clit,
You can swallow this dick!
I'll fuck ya sideways, baby,
Deeper than your pussy permits!

I'll fuck ya standin' up,
While you slap my face and curse!
Cry and Scream all you wish,
It'll only make it worse.

Beg for mercy all you want!
Beat on my chest, on my back you may claw!
But take a deep breath, a deep dick, and take this fuckin'!
Take it all!!! **<u>And TAKE IT RAW!!!</u>**

Slippery When Wet

Some call it a warning,
To others it's a threat.
To me, it's erotic perfection....
Slippery When Wet.

Hell yeah, she gotta slide & glide when she rides,
This dick that's as hard as it can get.
Nature's Motor Oil, Seductive Lubrication....
Slippery When Wet.

To see her body shine, just blows my mind,
When she's hot, and dripping with sweat.
I'm so damn thirsty, I wanna swallow every drop....
Slippery When Wet.

I want to slither up your body, consuming all as I go,
Your thighs, clit, nipples, and breasts.
My thirst is never ending, your river never stops flowing,
Slippery When Wet.

Damn! It's all I can think about,
But we just said hello, we just met!
I can't help it, I'm a man and I wanna shout,
I love a woman
who's Slippery When Wet.

Bitch

Are you tired,
After your hard day?
Well squeeze my dick!
And make me pay!

Is your Boyfriend on the phone,
With a fucked up call?
Then choke my collar !
And make me FALL!!

Push me on the floor,
on my hands and kness!
Shove your pussy down my mouth!
And force me to please!

Yes owner, your pussy's the bomb,
The best I'll ever get !
Please cum all over my tongue,
Or I ain't shit !

Kick my ass !
I'm your slut !
Beat me down !
While you MAKE me fuck !

My Tongue, Lips, Mouth, and Dick.......
You own all that I am....
Cause I'm......
YOUR BITCH !!!

The Speakeasy

The Speakeasy.

New Orleans in July, where freedom of speech and thought are not rights, but a lifestyle. The club is called the Speakeasy, where local folks come in to relax, listen to the live bands play, and more importantly, share their thoughts. Every Saturday night from 9 pm to 2 am, the Speakeasy holds what they call a "Speak your mind" session, where everyone is invited to come up on stage, read poems, tell stories, or just unload the burdens of a heavy week. A literal show and tell of humanity. All the patrons are family, all the customers are friends. It's the Starbucks of the soul crowd, a deep gathering of open minds.

One woman in particular, Zan, has a tremendous amount of talent. Zan can sing with the soul of slaves. But her real talent lies in her writing. In her writings, the poems she reads tell of her tribulations in life. Writing is her way to vent, her way to let go all off the wrongs that have been bestown upon her, and her way to share with the world all the blessings she receives. All who listen to her appreciate all she has to say, but not all understand what causes such a pretty woman to speak such heartfelt emotions and tribulations, save one man, Pierre.

Pierre has listened to Zan now every week for four months. He can't wait to come down to the club and hear what she has to say about her life, or how she feels about life in general. Pierre has figured out what no others in the club have, that her stories, her readings, her poems, are not just a random accumulation of thoughts and words, but a well laid out roadmap. A roadmap of her life. Everything she goes through, she shares with all. To Pierre, Zan is an open book, every week is left as a cliffhanger, and he can't wait to see what will happen in her life next. Zan doesn't know it, but the man that understands her most in the world, that feels her pain, sorrow, and joys, more than any other in her past or her present, is a stranger she has never met. Her true best friend, is nothing but a face in the crowd, another set of eyes, in an ocean of on-lookers.

Pierre shows up this week, anxious to hear what Zan has to say about her new love. For the last few weeks her writings have been of love and happiness. She would have a sort of giddiness about her as she read. He loved to see her so happy. He would smile from ear to ear as she read, and he could feel her contentment in life. She is a regular, so she gets to go on at the same time every Saturday, 12 midnight. It's about 11:30 and Pierre is watching her stand by the bar, talking to the bartenders. She is smiling, but not as happy as she has been. He wonders what is wrong, if anything, and he can't wait to find out. Finally, it's 12, and the stage is clear for her to talk to him.

The club is beautiful. Candle-lit tables, and a tall wooden stage in the middle of the room with a long walkway so you can smile as you walk by all your local friends. Pierre always stands in the standing-room-only section by the back bar. He likes to be able to stare at her without being obvious to anyone. He has to really watch her face; her eyes, her body language, her whole self, tells the story, along with her words. The past few weeks she's been literally running to the mic, smiling, flashing that gorgeous smile. This week, she walks, not looking at anyone on the way, just staring at the mic at the end of the runway. There she stands, slender, her hair pulled back, big round eyes, lowered half way, sleepy with sadness. "Hello, everyone. Happy to see all of you came out to share with me tonight. You know, we all got questions, questions in our minds. But tonight, it's not the questions in my mind I'm concerned with. It's the questions on men's minds I want to address." A few women clap and laugh. "Can y'all feel me, ladies? I mean, I know you wonder, WHAT THE HELL WAS HE THINKING?! You know, it's hard to understand a man, I know. But we all play the game, let's be honest girls. As we go to the store, and slip on that tight-ass dress, we look in the mirror, we look at our ass, right? We wonder if it's gonna get these boys jockin'!" Now she has all the women in the club either cracking up, clapping, or just kind of smiling away cause they are in a tight dress with a man they just pulled. "But right now, I'mma tell you what's on their minds. I'mma tell you from the time they say hello, to the time they hit, what's up with both those heads they think with. This poem is called, THE QUESTIONS OF MAN. Thank you very much, I hope you feel me. "

THE QUESTIONS OF MAN

What's your name?
Where you live?
What's your number?
How many kids?

Are they real?
Are they fake?
Go to a movie?
Go on a date?

Can I kiss you now?
Can I suck on your tits?
Does she go down?
When can I hit!?

Does she swallow?
Will she ride it bare?
Will she fall in love with me?
Why should I care?

Above are the Questions of Man,
Us women are shit outta luck.
Cause the only real question on their minds is,
WHO ELSE CAN I FUCK?

The room stays silent as she still holds the mic stand, caressing it, not letting go. "Again, thank you." and she walks away. The crowd is clapping, but it is soft. All that are there understand what she has said to a degree, they have been faced with the fact that we live a shallow existence for the most part. The men in the club that are thinking the very same thoughts she has just spoken of are mad that their game for the night has been crushed.

But Pierre, he is thinking of her spoken words as if she were trying to tell him directly, the frustrations she is having in her current relationship. He watches her body language as she walks off the stage. She is upset, troubled, walking off the stage swiftly, not looking back. He starts to analyze her words right away, he sees that the whole poem was dedicated, in chronological order, to the turmoil between her and her man. A time line of issues she is dealing with. And the last statement, **"Cause the only real question on their minds is, WHO ELSE CAN I FUCK?"** *Did he cheat on her, or was he* *going to, and they had it out. Is he that unhappy with her? What did he do? What actually happened? How can this man not be in love with her? She is perfect! Tall, beautiful, and intelligent! What is wrong with him?* Pierre can't wait for all these questions to be answered, hopefully next week when she will speak again. Until then, he will just spend his week doing the usual, same old thing: work, TV, sleep, a date on Thursday or Friday maybe, but always keeping Zan in his mind.

Finally it's Saturday again. Once again, in the Speakeasy, it's 11:45 pm, Zan will be up soon, and he sees her walk over to the bar as she always does to get her drink and talk to the bartender before she goes up. She always orders the same drink, Midori and Seven Up. She never strays from her routine, first her drink a short time before she goes on, a little small talk, then she's up. He studies her mannerisms before she goes up. He can see her big, beautiful eyes, mad, almost pensive, like she can't wait to get her chance to speak her mind. Then it's her time to talk to him again, 12 o'clock, midnight.

"Welcome once again to the Speakeasy, my name is Zan for those who don't know me. Ladies, it is now 12 o'clock, the *bewitching* hour." She pauses and looks across the room, looking slowly at each and every face, every pair of eyes, to make sure her next point is going to be received and understood. The silence is eerie, the combination of the dark club and the smoke-filled room has given the club a graveyard effect. "This is the time that men can cast their spell upon us. The time where all the lies can sound so real. When the alcohol has sedated our common sense, when the only thing we can think about is the brotha's perfect smile, his sexy voice, and

how long it has been since we last had it thrown on us good. You hear what I'm sayun?!" The women are laughing a little, leaning to whisper to their girlfriends about what Zan just said. "But beware ladies, I say beware! The game is dangerous, no matter how good it sounds, nothing comes free, and the things you thought were free, they take it all back when the game is ova! You never know who's telling the truth, so I cast this spell of common sense upon the women in the club tonight......"

She speaks as if reciting an incantation......

Truth or Dare

Beware this game,
Of Truth or Dare.
The lies they tell,
To hide the affair.

A man of truth,
Good will and prayer.
Can play yo' ass,
He will, I swear.

They say they love you,
You're special, they care.
But they'll break your heart,
Beyond repair!

The men of wealth,
With cars and flair.
Won't buy you shit!
They never share.

I preach the truth,
To warn, to scare.
They'll strip your soul,
And leave none to spare.

Heed my warnings, my sistas,
For now you are aware.
To beware this game,
Of Truth.......or Dare.

"Thank you." And with that, she walks slowly off the stage. The crowd is giving her love, the men are clapping because they liked her style, but the women are clapping because they heard her words. Pierre laughs because he knows the "Wanna-roll-my-Benz?" line ain't gonna work for these fellas this evening.

Ok, what was she really saying. Pierre starts to break the poem down immediately; he wants to understand what she meant. Maybe tonight he will have the nerve to approach her. Tonight was full of useful information about what happened to her. He has to understand the whole picture before he approaches her. He is captivated by this woman, and he doesn't want to blow his one chance to make that first impression. He thinks to himself, *Let's see...**The lies they tell to hide the affair,** ok, he played on her! That was easy to figure out, damn, how could he do that?? She's so perfect! Damn, he's a idiot! **A man of truth, good will and prayer...Can play your ass, he will, I swear!** OK, I bet he was a church-going man, probably one of those brothas that always said how he was stable and couldn't stand players!* (Now Pierre is getting mad thinking about the rest) ***They say they love you, you're special, they care****...ok, pretty easy here too, that's an old story, love 'em and leave 'em.* ***The men of wealth with cars and flair, won't buy you shit, they never share****. He had money, and she probably had to go without new stuff for herself. He no doubt*

kept her on lockdown, using the money as a way to try to control her. Often times men with money think money controls everything, and since they have it, they have all the power, just a bunch of control freaks! ***They'll strip your soul, and leave none to spare****...wow, he really hurt her. Damn, she must have really loved him. I gotta do something, I gotta talk to her! Wait....not now, not tonight, she's too mad right now, this is not the time, no way. Anything I say tonight is going to be taken wrong, and that will forever brand me as wrong; once ya push up wrong, it can never be right. I can't wait till next week. That's when I'll say something, Next week is my week!*

All week, Pierre thinks about the coming Saturday. He thinks of the situation. How will he approach her? He knows her routines, but he doesn't know what her demeanor will be. She might come back up and say she got back with her man, but he doubts that because she is of strong mind and will; she wouldn't go back to a bad situation once she has left. So he figures that he will just wing it, and be honest with her. Whatever he says to her, will be honest, that way, if he succeeds or fails, he will know he won't have to second guess what he did. So with that being decided, he couldn't stop thinking about this guy that played on her. *What the hell was his problem!? I mean, she is everything a man could hope for, what could another woman offer him that Zan can't fulfill!?* He uses the rest of that week pondering that exact question, until 11:45 pm Saturday night, at the Speakeasy.

Zan is at the bar again. Getting her Midori and Seven. She is laughing a bit, not a laugh of enjoyment, but more like a "I-cant-believe-this-shit" kind of laugh. She's being very sarcastic in her mannerisms. He can't wait to hear what's

going on. And then finally, it's midnight.

"Welcome to the Speakeasy, my name is Zan. You know what, ladies? Sometimes you can't win, you just can't win. You can do all the above on his list of things his perfect woman would do. You can shave your legs every dayum mornin'. You can keep your own job, run all his errands, keep the house clean, have dinner ready when he gets home, fuck him the way he wanna be fucked, suck his dick the way he likes it sucked, and even swallow that shit when he cums. And you know what? It still don't matter! A man's gonna be a man regardless, he's gonna fuck up on ya. It's just his way I guess. But I found out why my man did me wrong. Get this, there was an actual reason why I got mine. It all had to do with the OTHER bitch........here's my story..."

THE OTHER

The OTHER reason,
The OTHER one,
The OTHER person,
He made cum.

The OTHER night,
In the OTHER bed.
With the OTHER heffa,
That gave him head!

He came back that night,
In his OTHER draws.
Makin' OTHER excuses,
For the OTHER calls.

He pulled that OTHER bitch,
With that OTHER line!

I reminisce of the OTHER day,
When my man, was mine.

What do I do, ladies?
I can't do shit!
Cause my man's OTHER bitch...
GOT A DICK!

"Be careful out there sistas, ya neva know nowadays. And if it happens to you, understand that there is nothing you could have said or done to help your situation. Don't let that one man stop you from being happy. Whenever you feel like a man has gotten you down, keep your head up. You're worth betta and you'll find betta. I'm out peoples, have a good one, and thank you again."

Pierre just stands there, amazed. He can't believe that her man had another man! *No way! Well, it would explain a lot, it would explain how he could ruin such a good relationship, some urges can't be repressed for too long, I guess. Now is the time. She's said she'll find a better man, that means she's not overly bitter towards men, and she's keeping an open mind.* As Zan is heading back to the main bar, Pierre heads on an intercept course. He reaches the bar before her, and sees that she's been held up by some women that wanted to tell her how they liked what she said, how they felt her words. So he figures he can't just stand there waiting for her, he'll look like a stalker. So he calls the bartender over. "Midori and Seven please, make it the way Zan likes it." The bartender smiles as he might have been the only person in the place to notice that Pierre has had serious interest in Zan for over four months now. "Sure thing, partna," the bartender says, "this one's on me, go for yours." As he hands him the drink, Pierre turns around to see Zan almost bumping into him. "Oh, excuse me," he says, startled by Zan's sudden approach. She was coming to order her usual. Zan slides next to Pierre, leans on the bar, saying, "Hit me up!" This was her way to order when she came off the stage. "He's already got you covered, boo," said the bartender, smiling and pointing to Pierre, who slides her drink over to her.

"I knew you would need a drink after that one," Pierre said. They shared a small laugh. "You know what? I have to ask you a question right off the top, where do you get the courage to go up on stage and share your life with us all like that? I mean, you have a precious gift in your words, you move a lot of people, including myself. But why share your life with us so intimately? Oh, by the way, my name is Pierre." He smiles and sees that Zan is surprised by his sudden question, but she answers, "Well, to tell you the truth, I do it to vent. I have to get it out, and this is my way to express myself. I don't feel like I have a true partner in life that will listen to me, ya know. So I come here, to talk to everyone. I guess I will until I find that right someone. Wait.....you mean you actually realize that everything I've said was actually happening to me? Most people just figure I make it up every week from nowhere. They take it as entertainment value only." Pierre senses this is the moment he's been waiting for.

"Actually, to tell you the truth......wait, do you mind if we sit down somewhere we can talk a little more private? You know, there's a table right back there."

"Sure, no problem, I gotta hear this." So the two go back to one of the secluded candle-lit tables in the back on the club. "Now, you were saying...you were telling me the truth...continue." "Well, in truth, I felt as though you were speaking to me every week you've been up there for the past three weeks. Ever since the Questions of Man, I've been wanting to fill the void that was left in your life. Every week I though about what you said, like you were up there telling me, directly, what you needed in your life, and well, I couldn't wait to talk to you. I couldn't wait to tell you that your cries for a mutual and true love have been heard.. I know this is a lot coming from a stranger, but you're not a stranger to me. I feel as though I know you, at least I know some of what you've been through."

Zan is totally taken aback by Pierre. This man actually listened and paid attention to the point that he was putting it all together. She had to find out more about him; he already knew a lot about her. "Look Pierre, I normally leave right about now, and go grab a bite, wanna join me? You seem pretty cool, I got some things I wanna talk to you about. We can talk a little, you know, see what we really have in common." Pierre tries as hard as he can to keep cool. He wants to jump up and yell, but he doesn't want to seem desperate or crazy. "That sounds great, guess I get to find out what your favorite food is, as well as your favorite drink." Zan stops for a second, saying, "Yeah, how did you know what to order me to drink?"

"Well, let's just say I really pay attention, and leave it at that for now."

"Fair enuff, but you gonna tell me more, eventually." Pierre smiled at the word *eventually*, implying that there is going to be a lot more contact between the two. As they walk past the bar, the bartender and Pierre exchange looks; Pierre, a look of thanks to him, and the bartender, a look that said "Handle yo' business". This time, the bartender would have to wait till next week to see what happened on their little date.

Soon, it's Saturday, 11:45 pm, and Zan is at the bar. The bartender is pumping her for information, but she says he's gonna have to wait till she goes up and speaks, to find out what happened. He sees Pierre over in the back, as usual, then Pierre heads over to the owner. *What is he saying? Oops, time for Zan to go on.*

"Good evening. You know what? I gotta come on and thank you all for supporting the establishment, and the poets that come up here every week. I know that me, myself, I love coming down here and sharing with you all...and this poem, is dedicated to you."

Thank You Speakeasy

You've all been my extended family,
As week after week I've spoken my mind.
But now I bid a fond farewell,
As I speak my mind, one last time.

Remember the Questions of Man,
Brothas keep one woman, don't worry bout the rest.
It's about love, sharing, and commitment,
It's NOT all about the sex.

The playas game of Truth or Dare,
Ladies, a lying man is never worth the price.
There's never been a winner in a game full of lies,
Take heed to these warnings, and my advice.

When will we finally be able to stop worrying about THE OTHER?

The OTHER women or sometimes the OTHER men.
Life is a journey, best traveled by lovers,
Not a little boy's game, to lose or win.

So now I've spoken my mind,
And I've made my stand!
No more fake boys!
I've found a true MAN!

Thank you Speakeasy,
For fulfilling my dire need.
A true man that I can love,
And that same man....loving me.

"Thank you all once again. If the need ever arises for me to speak my mind, I'll be back on this stage to tell the tale. But hopefully, I'll get to stay amongst y'all down there. I wanna be a face in the crowd, supporting the artists, and living a happy life. So, with that being said..." The bar owner appears on stage and interrupts Zan. He takes the mic, "We have a special treat for Zan, since it is your last time, someone else, wants to speak his mind." And Pierre walks on stage, smiles at Zan, takes the mic, and faces her, holding her hand.

My Gift

I share this stage with you,
As now I share my life.
The patrons saw you as entertainment,
I viewed you as a wife.

Every week I fell deeper in love,
As I watched you speak your mind.
Your emotions shared for all to hear,
And my heart broke, with every line.

I would stand back and watch in disbelief,
As your life unfolded in rhyme.
Thinking of how I would make you happy and complete,
If I could only make you mine.

So on this stage, I'll call cloud nine,
I stand here next to you, finally complete.
You've given me the gift of taking care of your needs,
The gift of acceptance,
Thank you, for accepting me.
I love you.

"Thank you all, thanks to this place, we have found each other. And he hands the mic to the owner. They kiss on stage and walk off to roaring applause. They head toward the bartender, and Pierre orders for both of them, " One Midori and Seven, and two straws." Then Zan butts in, "Make that two Midori and Sevens. Don't get too happy now, shit, I'll share my life....but not my drink, nigga, back da hell up!" They both laugh and take their drinks, and as they sit down, Zan takes the straw from Pierre's glass, and puts it in hers, as they share their first drink of many, at the Speakeasy.

82

Wicked

Pleasures™

PASSION

Uncontrollable fire,
Blazing through my soul!
Lust, yearnings, desire,
ALL outta control!

My heart beating outta my chest!
Wanting to pump with all that I am, and nothing less.
To start a journey, of hours on end,
A trip down ecstasy, destination...Sin.

To never be finished,
To never be done.
To sex my woman down,
To melt with her cum.

Hell yeah, all of these are one in the same,
Cause I let it all out, I never ration.
All are components of one whole,
All of the above, assemble...Passion.

YOUR SERVER

Hello, what can I get you this evening,?
What are you in the mood for? Tell me, what do you wanna feel?
May I suggest an appetizer of foreplay,
Always a great way to start your meal.

I'll be your server for the evening,
I'm here to fulfill all your needs.
Grade A service, an Orgasmic Chef,
So leave a tip, if you please.

Our Special tonight....exquisite,
A dick that never gets soft.
Then a five-star fuckin' as your main course,
Guaranteed to get you off.

As always, your choice was excellent,
I'm glad you've enjoyed your little stay.
Let me wash my Face & Hands, and thank you,
Please, pay the cashier along your way.

I hope you visit me again real soon,
Just call me up, let me know when.
So I can satisfy all your appetites, oh, and...
Thank You, Please, Cum Again.

<u>Service With A Smile</u>

Welcome to my service station,
What'll it be today?
Service with a smile, baby,
Oh, <u>I'll fill you up</u>, right away!

First time to my station?
I understand if you're nervous.
Turn the lights a little lower, and enjoy yourself,
You can watch me, self service.

But Full Service is my specialty,
Total inspection from head to toe.
Rotate that ass, and a deep-down lube,
Check your fluids, make 'em flow.

Oh my goodness! What do we have here?
<u>Orgasmic Build-Up!</u> You haven't come in a while!
Satisfaction guaranteed, as I'll take care of that problem,
And as always, Service With A Smile.

YOU ARE WHAT YOU EAT

Baby wake up, I'm hungry.
Come on boo, just gimmie a lil' snack.
Don't worry baby, I'll do all the work,
All you gotta do is roll ova' on your back.

Don't fuss, just gimmie what I need,
Cum real quick, then go back to bed.
Your thighs are shakin' and ya' buckin up and down....
Oooohhh that's it baby, GRAB the back of my head!

When you're sweating, shaking, and catching your breath,
You lay there looking so fine.
My balanced meal baby, Recommended Daily Value,
Top Choice Certified, GRADE A PRIME!

You left for work with that glow,
And you had that bounce in your step.
As soon as we get back home,
You know what you're gonna get.

But a funny thing happened as I passed the candy store,
Thinking how I needed to get home for my treat.
I bumped into a man, and he called me a PUSSY!
I just smiled and said, You Are What You Eat.

Grown Man

From Sperm to a Man,
Such as a seed to a tree.
Cultivated in this concrete jungle,
I stand the man I was *Grown* To Be!

My parents instilled in me values,
To keep me grounded, connected to my roots.
But ill-trusted women have raided me like locusts,
Milking the sap from my body, raping me of my fruits.

Oh, all the seductive gardeners,
Saying how they were different from ones in the past.
How they will nourish me to be strong once again,
How they had the formula to make us last.

Ummm, the fond memories,
How they would climb on my every limb.
Straddling my branch in between their thighs,
As we shared in the fruits of sin.

But as the seasons changed, one fact remained,
The destiny of a tree, they were gonna leave.
But how many times can I live through this cycle,
Greet, Love, Hate, always deceived.

Ladies, men are results of what your sisters have grown,
So when we judge you, don't ask why.
We might be straight up, twisted, mangled, or shady,
But y'all grew these men, so don't cry.

So here I stand,
Bending without breaking, as far as I can.
If earth holds a tree, then let a good woman be my land!
I am a product of all before me,
Here I stand, a *Grown* Man!

CLOSURE

Closure

The story starts with the slam of a door on the second story of a two story apartment building.

<SLAM!! Footsteps stomping down the stairs>: "

Baby....come on...what is it???? Whatever I did, I'm sorry, what's wrong.....come back up baby, don't leave.

It's Tyree again, begging his girlfriend Sirauon not to leave. The neighbors downstairs have seen this over and over like clockwork...twice a month, they go through this. Sirauon is a very beautiful woman, five foot ten, slim, but with a great body. Tyree is a equally beautiful man, 6'3, very athletic, and every bit as fine as his woman. Tyree has a good career, owns his own business; Sirauon is trying to become a model, and believes with all her heart she will make it....she just needs someone to understand her and be a " Strong Man " until she makes it big.

They make a stellar couple, to see them together is a beautiful sight. But other than their physical appearance, they are polar opposites. Tyree loves Sirauon with all his heart...all he wants to do is settle down and get married. He is a very, " Good Man ". Good values, never cheats on his love, and always puts the needs of his loved ones before his own. Sirauon on the other hand, feels as though that is what she is owed for being beautiful. But if you ask about their relationship at one of their little get togethers, she'll tell you how she stands behind her man and supports him. Its the same story over and over again, all about the time when Tyree was sick and she played nursemaid to him. " Oh yeah, he was a big baby...but I got up at 2 in the morning and got him some orange juice, but that's my baby, and that's just how I am." Once in their two year relationship, she catered to him and helped him. She uses that as a sort of validation, a re-assurance she is a good woman. < Now that you know our couple...>

Sirauon is stomping down the stairs, and Tyree is trying with all his heart to not go after her this time. As always he fails, and goes running after her, trying to reach her before she gets to her car. She sees him coming, she knows he's coming, she has his routine down, she gets in her car and drives off with her sunglasses on, not even lookin in his direction. On the long, lonely walk back to his apartment, he thinks to himself, " Why do I go through this, she doesn't really love me, she does this to me on purpose, that's it, no more!!! She's out!!! I'mma pack her things she has upstairs, and dropping it off on her doorstep, it's OVER!!! " He's thought these same thoughts every time this has happened, and all he ever does is end up blaming himself for her tantrums. He cusses himself out for being so weak, but in reality, he is just in love. He is a giver, and she, is the classic taker.

As he approaches his stairs, his downstairs neighbor Ron, asks him if he's ok. Ron and Vita are a great married couple downstairs, who are good friends with Tyree, and really understand how he loves Sirauon, but doesn't need to be with her. They have had little heart to heart talks with him before, after some of these fights, but no matter how much since they have made, he always takes her back, or goes begging back himself. But as a good friend, Ron is worried about him. " Is this it dog??? Is it final??? ", Ron asks. In reply, Tyree just lowers his head to hide the coming tears, and says what he always does, " It aint really nothin' dog, she's just trippin a

little." And he goes upstairs.

Normally Ron leaves it at that, but this time, on this day, Ron tells Vita, and they decide to have a little get together to get Tyree out of his apartment. So he wont have to sit alone, and feel sorry for himself, or God forbid, go out and spend up all his money on gifts to cheer Sirauon up. So Ron goes up to Tyrees place and tells him to come on down in a hour or so and kick it, and Tyree says he'll be down. In the mean time, Vita is on the phone calling a few of her girlfriends over, single, and married, and Ron is inviting his boys over.

Its about 7pm when everyone starts arriving. All in all about 20 people are invited for a nice night of cards, movies, music, and just talking about what has happened to them since their last get-together. Tyree is still upstairs, and is almost ready when he hears the people getting louder, saying hello and such. He look out the window and gets sort of excited to see that others were invited. " Better iron these pants...damn I wanna hurry up and get down there though, no, I gotta look like I have a life." Once Tyree has everything together, he grabs some wine and beer from the fridge and heads downstairs. He's met a lot of the people there before, and re-introduces himself. The atmosphere is very warm and fun. Everyone is really enjoying themselves, the couples are having a great time, and the single people are sharing things in common. Tyree just stops for a moment, and looks around; noticing everyone there is smiling except for one girl. She is talking to people that approach her, but her smile is forced, and she just keeps staring at the T.V, she concentrates on the T.V so hard that it is obvious she's trying to keep herself out of the party. So feeling sort of out-of-place himself, considering he's neither single or married, but he has a girlfriend, and doesn't, he goes to sit by her. "Hey, hows it goin'?" he says. " Fine ", and that's all she has to say, a quick smile, and back to the TV. Of all things, she's watching cartoon network, and Tyree is a cartoon freak! Tyree makes comments about the cartoons, and she laughs, they start their own private game on what the next line in the cartoon is gonna be. Pretty soon they are having a lot of fun, and time is passing by really fast. After two hours or so, the two are sitting really close, she has leaned into his shoulder, and his arm is up on the back on the couch, almost wrapped around her. They start talking about their favorite movies of all time, and what they were doing, at the time they saw them. This really breaks any tension that was left, they totally have all the same movies in common, and seemingly, a lot of the same memories related to those moments. It's now going on 11pm, and the couples are going home, its Sunday night, gotta work tomorrow. But the single people are still there. Ron and Vita are good sports and everyone there are good friends, so they tell everyone left, not to worry, they are in it for the night, don't worry about them, and to have fun. Vita sees Tyree with sitting with her friend Taress. She knows Taress is in a really bad relationship, and seeing Tyree and her together is giving her hope. She knows they would be great together. They are both loving, caring individuals. Ok, given, Taress aint Sirauon, Taress is only about 5'7" and is a little " Thick ", but she is cute, and is a great person. So in her excitement, Vita runs to Ron and tells him to go get his CD's from the bedroom. Vita and Ron are really into the oldies, and they bring out the Whispers CD. At first it was cool, but 3 songs into it, people were going out to their cars ta get their favories slow jam cds, and

any other music that could get someone in the mood to do things with someone they don't know.

So Tyree tells Taress that he has some new CDS upstairs. Her face lights up and tell him to go get em'. Now Tyree knows exactly where to find em' upstairs cause he had it all set up for him and Sirauon, they are still loaded in the CD player, which is connected to the light switch on the wall. When the lights are cut on, the CDS will play, he liked things to be romantic. So, Tyree gets up from the couch, and he smiles as he notices his shoulder feels cold now, cause Taress' head had been there for the last 3 hours keeping it warm; sometimes it's the little things. When Tyree gets ready to go upstairs, Taress decides to go with him, she doesn't want to be downstairs with the " Mackin " going on, and she feels a lot more comfortable with him. She looks around to tell Vita, but she's no where to be seen, either is Ron. But she really trusts Tyree so she just says, " Wait up, can I come with you, I don't want nobody down here comin up ta me as soon as you leave, you know how peeps can get." Tyree feels like a big kid, he's all happy that Taress wants to spend time with him. It's been a long time since he's had someone really want to spend time with him. Imagine, this woman doesn't even want him to leave the room without her. It melts his heart.

So, they leave the party, and walk upstairs. A little small talk on the way up, usual stuff, " I hope you like my little place, I know I need to dust." ect. They get to the door, he stands aside so she can enter, then he does it, he hits the light switch. The CD was already cued up and ready to play, and the music starts playing. "I never heard this one before, but it sounds good as hell." Tyree looks at her, sitting there on the

couch, and he doesn't see a woman 4 inches shorter and 20 ponds heavier than Sirauon, he sees a sweet, soft, caring woman, who has a soft heart, and very full lips. But he thinks of Sirauon, even though he's feeling this natural, real bond with Taress, he does still have a girlfriend, or does he? She did leave him. He almost forgets that just a few hours ago he was crying over her, totally depressed. Now he's happier than he has been in a long while. And he feels more comfortable with Taress than he ever has with Sirauon. So Tyree tells himself right then and there," Don't let her go without getting her number! " No matter what happens, get the number!!! Tyree goes to sit next to Taress, and he sits on the last cushion of the couch, by the arm. Taress is sitting in the middle, and asks Tyree if she can have some water. " Course' sweetie, and off he goes into the kitchen." When he comes back, Taress look at him and says, " Do you have another bottle of that wine we had downstairs??? Weren't you the one that brought it??" Now Tyree is putting things together in his mind, " hmmmm if she noticed I brought the wine, that means she was paying attention to me from the jump." " Yeah, I'm sure I do," Tyree goes to the fridge and pulls out the bottle that was intended for Sirauon that night. Why not, Taress is much better company anyway, " I hope I don't mess this up, don't read anything into it, just have fun." " Here you go! " but this time, when he come back, Taress is right next to the spot where he first sat, suggesting they resume where they left off downstairs. Things are going very well indeed.

As they cuddle, and sip on wine, Tyree starts to hold her glass while she drinks, he notices how perfect her lips are. He loves the way she looks up and smiles at him every time she

gets just enough, and he pulls the glass away. Now the CD is halfway through playing, and they are in the full cuddle position. Tyrees legs are both on the couch, and Taress's whole body is in between his legs, with her back on his stomach, and her head on his chest. He is smelling her hair, its so clean, so simple, not like the heavy, designer label shampoo Sirauon uses. He wants to kiss her so bad. How to do it? He goes thought it over and over in his mind. Does he move and mess up their position??? It would be a labor to do, but it would be romantic to get on his knees and kiss her. No, that would take to long, getting up, making her lose her position, then what if she rejects him, or gives him a mercy kiss because she likes him, but not in," that way." No he has to do something, if its right, she'll understand. So he opts for something in the middle, he sits up a bit, leans down, and kisses her on the side of the cheek. And immediately she smiles, " ummmmm ". She puts her hand on his inner thigh. So he pulls her hair back a bit, and kisses her on her neck, many small soft kisses. After every kiss, in rhythm, she is stroking his thighs, purposely trying to get a specific, primal, reaction. The dynamics have changed. Now both of their hearts are racing. He whispers in her ear, " I am so glad you are here, you make me feel better than I have in a long time. You are so beautiful. " Taress stops, and turns all the way around. Her 40 B chest pressed against his body. She look him in his eyes and says, " You are truly a beautiful man. " they stare at each other for a short time, he softly touches her face, tracing the contours of the cheeks, and Taress crawls up his body and they kiss for the first time. The kiss is very raw, but a genuine affection is felt. Their two bodies are pressed hard against each other, the turn on is

amazing for both of them. Tyrees hands are on her back, and she grabs them and slides them down to her ass. Now its really on!!! They are into heavy petting when out of no where, Taress starts to cry.

This no doubt comes as a shock to Tyree, so, still breathing heavy, he feels bad, like he did something. He's scared now, thinking he really messed up. But Taress tells him that she just got dogged by a man who is wrong for her, but she never has the strength to stay away from him. She tell Tyree that she's sorry, but she still feels a lot of anger towards this man. Tyree just look at this wonderful woman, crying, showing on the outside, the same way he feels inside. He doesn't know why, but he feels a bond, a connection with this woman that makes him know, she'll understand what he is about to do.

He takes her hand, and tells her, " Follow me sweetie, I have something I want to show you. You have to see this, you have to know that I understand you, and you are not alone in life." Tyree takes her to the closet where only Sirauon's things are, and shows her the luggage underneath the hanging clothes. " We broke up today, again, for the um-teenth time, she uses me, but I can never pack her things." A moment hits them both, Taress stops crying, and they both start to laugh. " We are truly sad " she says. " I never thought anyone else felt like I do, much less a man!!!" "Well, I do, but you know what, since I been with you tonight Taress, I haven't felt sorry for myself. It actually helped me to see clearly what I have been doing to myself, thank you baby, I mean that, thank you." Taress walks up to Tyree, smiles, puts her finger on his mouth to quiet him, " Fuck em both! " she says. " They wont ruin this night!!!, Don't take this wrong, but I think we both feel it. We got a lot of anger, and we need to express it. So lets express our asses off. This shit is gonna be therapy!!!! I gotta get this anger outta me somehow or I'll never let him go, and you have to find the strength to do whats best for you too. I need to hate you right now!!! I'm gonna do whats I feel is best for me for a change!!! Hell yeah!! Fuck him!!! And FUCK her!!!! I need to hate you, and FUCK you like I hate you! And you need to do the same. Take it all out on my ass, cause imma do the same to you!!!! You down???"

Tyree is really caught off guard, but for some reason, this woman can do no wrong by him. Everything she says sounds so right!!! So with that being said, it was war!!!!

She tried to push him against the wall, but he just picked her up as she wrapped her legs around him, and he carried her into the bedroom, passionate kisses the whole way! He didn't lay her down, he just fell on top of her, falling hard in-between her legs, but they never lost lip contact, still kissing...very hard! They were tearing at each other clothes!!! Going for the shirts while they were grinding on each other. He was so hard he felt like he was going to tear through is skin!!! And she was so wet he could feel her pants soaked, and it made his pants soaked enough for him to feel her wetness though his pants!! Then Taress expressed the anger she was talking about, " she flipped him off of her, and pinned him on his back. She pulled off his pants, and grabbed his hard dick with both her hands, " I'm so sick of your punk ass!!! I bet those bitches you cheated with didn't Fuck you like this!!! Now lay you punk ass down and don't say shit!!! " now Tyree really understood what was happening, and how it was gonna be, man this was great!! Taress stood above him, and pulled her pants off, leaving her panties on. She dropped down, right next to his face, her pussy right over his mouth, " Now eat through these panties bitch!!! Eat through these panties like the mutha fuckin dog that you are!!!! " Taress was really pissed!!! Tyree figures he's in this for the long haul, he better get into it, or things might really get messed up, plus, this was a liberating experience.

So he does what she orders, he's tearing through her panties, making the hole bigger and bigger. When he has a whole big enough for his lips and his mouth to fit through, Taress stands up, takes whats left of her panties off, and drops back down on Tyrees face. Grinding hard into his lips. She's buckin back and forth, and he's sucking on her clit, massaging it in between his lips, and rolling it around on his tongue!! She feels herself ready to explode, and she tightens her thighs around his head, looks down and sees his helpless head in her pussy, pleasing her, and she is freed of all the anger she harvested when she cums all over his face. " ummmmmm baby......you taste so dayum good. " Taress relaxes, rubs her hands in his hair, and starts to catch her breath.

Tyree thinks to himself, " hell no, therapy is two way, not one, I could have ate out Sirauon for that matter. Ohhhhh hell naw!!!" As Taress relaxes, Tyree asserts himself, ver forcefully!! Now its his turn. "Oh, you think I'm just a weak nigga now huh??? Because I try to take care of your selfish ass, and give a Fuck about you?? Well now, your gonna take a FUCK!!! Your gonna lay your ass down and take this FUCK!!!" He doesn't enter he gently, no, he just puts all of himself in her hard and fast. She tries to slide back to ease it in, but he grabs her legs, and pushes her knees back to her ears!

Tyree is a strong man, very powerful, and he uses all of it against her. Taress just has to hold her breath and try to take it. He fucks her so hard that every time she closes her eyes, she can see bright flashes in her eyelids. She feels like she can hardly breath, he feels so deep. But he has no mercy. He doesn't lick her breasts while he fucks her, he bites them. She knows its almost over, she feels him speeding up, and growing even more inside her, she's screaming, and he's cussing her out, then he cums. He pulls out and explodes all over her neck. "You always said you wanted a pearl necklace bitch, there you are!!!" Then he collapsed next to her.

They were both quite for about 10 minutes, mostly catching their breath. They both got up and went to the bathroom, getting some mouthwash. Then came the talk afterwards. But it wasn't awkward as one might think. Taress just slipped on her pants, tossed on her shirt, and kissed him in the bed, saying only this, "Now that we've found each other, we needed this, without it, we would never have had closure.: If you feel the same, we can go on, but I know I can do what I have to do now baby, and I will always love you for that." Tyree kissed her back, and said, " I hated you this morning, can I love you tonight? " " Nine o clock baby, I'll be here " Taress smiles, gets her purse, and leaves. The sun was new, as the morning started. He walked her to her car, and she smiled at him as she drove away waving. Ron heard him come down the stairs and just gave him a smile and laughed at Tyree as he walked by his window.

An hour later Tyree walks back down the stairs, and Ron and Vita are on their way to work, walking to their cars. Tyree has the bags in his hands, and Vita asks him, " So whats up?"....." Finnaly getting rid of old luggage yall. Just cleanin house."

Wicked

110

Sustenance

When she touches me,
She feeds the tempest,
that is my passion.

A mere glance of her,
Fuels the fire,
that is my desire.

To kiss her,
is to pacify the lust that is rampant and primal.
But I must sacrifice immediate gratification,
For a love, that could be final.

To have her look at me,
with yearning in her eyes,
is to feed my soul,
and unbind its ties.

I want to consume her,
I want to love her.
In my heart, she is solitaire,
In my soul, there is no other.

I thank God she is my now,
I pray she shall be my tomorrow.
I shall starve in all these ways without her,
For she is my Sustenance.

RAIN

She was my only sunshine,
Without her, all I feel is pain.
Without her light, I suffer in clouds of loneliness,
And disappear, in her shadows of Rain.

With her, I was strong and proud,
Without her, I'm on the verge of going insane!
Be it in the middle of the day in July,
All my heart can see is her Rain.

She was my only inspiration,
Without her, I have nothing to gain.
I sit still with no motivation,
Floating endlessly in her Rain.

All my joy, pride, and life itself,
With one stroke, all has been slain.
I wasn't stabbed, shot, or crucified,
But I was drowned, in her Rain.

114

Perfectly Flawed

"My ass is too big!"
All the better ta bounce you with.
"My lips are too fat!"
All the better ta suck on when we kiss.

"My thighs are too chunky!"
I love the way they feel wrapped around my head.
"I think I'm too heavy!"
I get off on the squeaky sound we make in the bed.

"My nose is too wide!"
Baby when you cum that hard, ya gotta breathe!
"I think I'm too tall!"
Your pussy's right in my mouth when I'm on my knees.

Baby don't change a thing,
You're perfect the way you are.
You say you're black, dark as night.
I say, "At night, is when I can see the stars."

You see, your Vices are your Virtues,
You were sent to me from God!
God is perfect, He can do no wrong,
And God, has made you Perfectly Flawed.

A Bird In The Hand

You're my best friend, my rock,
My anchor, for the past 4 years.
We've shared each other's ups and downs,
Triumphs and Tribulations, joys and tears.

How many times was my heart broken,
How many times was I broken down??!!
How many times did you say "She's not worth it!"
"Don't worry, baby, your true love will be found!"

All those times we sat up all night,
Cause I was too depressed to sleep.
All those nights you told me to "Be Strong!"
"You will find that love that you seek!"

But you haven't found your husband yet,
As I, haven't found my wife.
We remained each other's "Somebody"
Together, through our "Somebody-Less" life.

On our 4-year anniversary,
As we reminisced about the loves that we missed.
We laughed as we confessed to one another,
We were always curious, about how each other kissed.

Then the laughing stopped,
2 am was the time.
That our friendship changed forever,
As your lips, touched mine.

My head started spinning
As I felt your tongue!
My Gawd, this can't be happening!
On my friend I can't get sprung!

Your body was so warm and loving,
As I laid you back, and climbed on top.
Then Fear & Love both consumed me,
You're my friend, I gotta stop!!

The war as old as man itself,
Mind against body, I had to fight!
"Baby, I've loved you for 4 years now",
"To do this tonight, just wouldn't be right!"

"Let's stop and think about what we're doing!"
"If we do this, it will never be the same!"
You said, *"I've been used and abused for so many years"*
"I want a man that loves me, to make love to me for a change."

I know all you've been through,
Just as well as you know me.
But let's give this a little more time, baby,
Just two more weeks, then, we'll see.

14 days by the Calendar!
336 hours by the Watch!
To the day that I'll be inside of you,
And act out my most loving, yet lucid of thoughts.

So as the sun rose, we made a pact.
Two weeks, nigga, then bring yo' ass back!
Oh, we're not gonna rush, I'mma take my time,
Half a month to the day, til yo' ass will be mine!

So with the agreement being reached,
And the arrangements being said.
I went home and called up Vegas,
To make the arrangements for our bed.

That first week was pure torture!

Could I make it? It was in doubt!
Then my homie, my boy, called ta save me.
" Yo' nigga.....let's go out."

" I ain't seen yo ass in a while,"
"Tonight is on me, don't even bring yo money."
"It's gonna be off da hook, gonna be wild!"
"You know how we do it, gonna be some honies!"

So I ironed my jeans,
And I'm out the door.
Been to a million parties,
What difference was one more?

As they say, "The party was jumpin'",
"And the place was packed."
Then oh my gawd, it happened,
She walked in, and she was Stacked!

Her eyes could see right through my soul,
Every feature was perfect, without flaw.
She walked with a confidence only a Queen would know!
As I stood there mesmerized, just in awe!

I shoulda known better,
From the very first sign.
Outta all the dicks in the room,
She HAD ta pick mine!

The conversation was nothing special,
Your average Hi, How ya doin', Hello.
Then she just walked up close, beside me,
Whispered in my ear, "Baby, let's go"

"Where you wanna go?"
"It doesn't matter, anywhere secluded and far."
So I drove up to the top of the hill,

Where she fucked me in my car!

She was everything I ever dreamed!
This woman was perfect, or so it seemed.
Her body was tight, a poster child for sin!
And when I came in her mouth, she just swallowed, and grinned.

"I gotta be getting back,"
"We been gone kinda long!"
I can't wait to tell my boy!
Man this shit was the bomb!

I looked at this woman,
And I knew I was done.
My search is finally over,
This one, **<u>was the one</u>**!

With that sense of gratification,
We started back on our ride.
Then my heart stopped, a hesitation,
As I felt the pain inside.

Oh my god,
What did I do.
I can't tell HER now,
Not after all we been through.

After all her heartbreak,
After all the times she's been dissed.
How could I hurt my friend so deep,
How could I just be another nigga on that list!

But I had to tell her the truth,
Never once have I ever lied.
But this time, what friend would she have to turn to,
As this time, I'm the man that would make her cry.

I waited the rest of that week,
I had to tell her, it's the last day.
I sat her down **on her packed suitcase**,
"Baby, I have something I gotta say."

As I told her the story,
The tears flowed from her eyes.
"I fell in love at first sight, boo,"
"I can't go without her, I apologize!"

FUCK-YOU!! GET-OUT!!!
I could hear the pain in her cries.
I lost the best friend in the world,
I could never come back, I realize.

I had never in life imagined,
Such a deep sense of loss.
Like my soul itself had been tortured,
Or crucified, on the cross.

I hadn't seen "Her"
Since that night.
I needed her more than ever now,
I needed love in my life.

I needed her reassuring comfort,
As I ran desperately to her arms.
I needed her to sedate my pain with her lovin'
To inject me with 100cc's of her charms.

But then the shock of my life she gave me,
Her reaction, I could NEVER foresee!
When she told me this time I'd have to pay for it!
She liked me, so the first fuck was FREE??!!!

I can't believe I was so blinded!
I can't believe I didn't know!
I can't believe I lost the love of a lifetime,
Over a HUNDRED-DOLLAR HOE!!!

LIPS

Lips that are hidden,
For which my tongue to glide.
Are the lips that bloom as a flower,
Just before I get inside....

Those lips that are pink,
Which make the men think,
Of makin' those lips red,
After a long night in bed.

Lips that are thin,
But with extreme skill.
Or the Lips that are fat,
With that wrap-around feel.

Lips can give a cold shoulder,
Those same lips can lick, and make ya hot.
Your lips read this poem,
As your lips speak my thoughts.

Lips that yell it's OVER!
As two lovers break apart.
But the lips that say I love you,
Those are the lips, that will keep my heart.

SHADOWS

IN THE SHADOWS LIES THE TRUTH

Karen had a long day today. She just broke up with her boyfriend Craig yesterday. Now she had to go through the day at work thinking about him, and trying not to get emotional. The time seemed to crawl by all day. She found herself looking at her watch every five minutes. Every time she heard the phone ring, she would have an ear open, waiting for it to be Craig, calling for her. But not even a salesman called her. But now she was home, alone, and she knew Craig wasn't coming over.

"What's the big deal", she thought. "He wasn't even fucking me anyway. We haven't had sex in 2 months! That's cause he was fuckin' that bitch!". But she stops there, and starts to cry, realizing how mad she was at him, but being more mad at herself, for still wanting him.

So it's off to the fridge fro a raid! Thinking to herself, "Hmmm lets see, check the freezer, any ice cream?? YES!!! Neapolitan, cool, all three flavors still left. What else, lemmie check the fridge!" But as she closes the door, she swears she sees a shadow out the corner of her eye. It makes her pause real quick, but then she figures its probably the image of the freezer light still in her eyes, playing tricks on her. So, she goes to the fridge....hmmmm a half bottle of wine!!! " Hell yeah, its on, lemmie put another one in now though, I know I'mma need it!" She closes the fridge, and there again, was that shadow she keeps thinking she sees, right out the far corner of her eye. No biggie, get the spoon, go the bedroom, and it's on.

She sticks the spoon in the ice cream container, picks

up the wine, and heads for her bedroom. She gets to her room, hits the power on the T.V., turns to the channel guide on cable to see whats on, and flops on the bed. It's dark in her room, the only light coming from the TV set. She kicks off her shoes, tosses her blazer on the hamper, and still in the rest of her work clothes, starts on the ice cream. Looking at whats available on cable tonight..." Hmmmm lets see, 10pm....HBO: Real SEX 18 !! COOL!! At least I'll see that someone is getting some! Fuck that, I'm gonna see some shit I'll do to my next man, that I never did with Craig!"

So she's watching the sexy program, eating her ice cream, and drinking her wine. By the Middle of the program, all her wine, and half the ice cream is gone. She's really into the show, so she runs into the kitchen, pops the cork on the other bottle of wine, and runs back to her room. She flops back on the bed, this time, not thinking about the ice cream, and just drinks the wine out of her bottle, watching the couples on the screen have wonderful sex. The women on the show seem to be getting so much pleasure! The men are totally into pleasing them, taking their time, caressing all parts of their body. She is getting VERY hot watching how the women build up into multiple orgasms, and the men just want to do more! Craig was never that way, he just came in, fucked her, made up some excuse, and left. She never even had a orgasm with him, she would always please herself when he left.

As the show goes off, she is wet and horny from all she saw. The room just has a glow from the TV, and she turns the sound off so she can concentrate on pleasing herself. As she strokes her clit, and plays with her pussy, she thinks about what she saw on TV. She thinks of how her next man is gonna do all the things she saw. As her orgasm builds up, she can imagine, and really see their heads buried into her pussy, swallowing her wetness. When her walls start to shake, she thinks of Craig eating her out, she thinks of MAKING him eat her out!! Of having total control of him!!! Then she cums, violently, and starts to catch her breath. And a little thought crosses her mind, "Was it me, or was the light in the room getting brighter while I was doing that???? It seems so dark now, but it seemed so bright a minute ago. Naw, probably just me trippin', whew, I gotta change these sheets."

As she changes her sheets, she looks at her room, its like the glare from the TV is giving the shadows life. As the TV scenes change, the light in the room changes, making the shadows dance, disappear and re-appear. She look at her room for a good minute, then feels the buzz from that wine really kick in, so she finishes up making her bed so she can go to sleep.

She settles in, realizing that Craig aint gonna call, but she doesn't care, she's to relaxed right now, and she falls off to sleep. In her dream, she dreams of her whole day, exactly as it happened, including the shadows she thought she saw in the kitchen. But this time, she saw them a little better, they weren't as fast. But she still ignored them. As she dreamt of watching the Sex on TV, the real point of the dream came to view.

The light of the TV flickered, as she just returned from getting her second bottle of wine, and this time, when she flopped on the bed, she looked at her own shadow, long and shapely on the bed. She stared at it, at its form, its shape, its curves. She glid her hands across the bed, like the shadow was

her partner, and she was touching the shadows hand. Then, she felt the shadow touch her. She pulled her hand back, startled! But the shadow didn't pull back with her, instead, it stayed on the bed, a perfect silhouette of herself. She was scared, but more fascinated than anything. She stared at her shadow for a while, she even rolled over and sat up, never taking her eyes off it, but it never moved. Just stayed, flat on the bed, mocking the position she was in earlier. Then it moved again. But this time, it was different. It was 2 dimensional, but it could raise off the bed. From the front she looked whole, like she was a image of herself, but from the side, she was flat, a thin black line. But it was nonetheless perfect. Not a blemish, perfect curves. The shadow touched her softly, sliding up the bed like spilled water. When its hands reached her, it was a feeling of perfect warmth. Not just on the surface of her skin, but all the way through, as the shadow slid up her legs, the warmth reached her shins, and she could feel it out the back of the calves. Up and up the shadow slid, melting inside of her, her pussy was already so wet from the show, she was ready for anything, she couldn't wait until it reached her clit!! When the shadow reached her pussy, she could feel the true nature of what it was, it was like pure energy. It had a steady feeling of vibration coursing through it, and now she was being slowly vibrated from the inside out! The vibrating since of power, the perfect warmness, the more excited she became, the more electricity the shadow gave off. The shadow was perfect, she understood, it would imitate her totally, the more she built up, the more excitement she gained, the more the shadow would give her! This was a perfect unison, soon the shadow was working its way up, past her belly button, spreading to her breast. She could feel the energy pulsating up her body, ticking her stomach, but never stopping the pleasure to the rest of her body, just spreading it.

As the shadow reached her breasts, she felt its warmth and energy envelop her breasts, massaging them perfectly from the inside, and the vibration pulsating on her nipples. Now her whole body was in extasy. This shadow had no needs of its own, its purpose was her pleasure, would it ever stop?? The shadow kept caressing her, fulfilling her, until it covered her whole body. As it rested totally over her body, she couldn't see it on her head or face, but it was there. She could hear a light, constant sound in her ears. Like a wave on electricity, of slow energy, moving in and out like waves on a quite night at the beach. It was very soothing, and allowed her to relax as she never has before. She just laid there and let herself be pleased totally, from the inside out, her whole body at once, it was almost to much to handle. As her orgasm built up. She could feel her whole body aflame with the energy, the sound in her ears was now like popping electricity wild, crashing building waves, bigger and bigger, the shadows sound was mocking the actual feelings of a building orgasm!!! This was too much! She could hear herself cumming too??!!!! Damn that was it, she had never felt anything like this before!!! Never had an orgasm been reached so perfectly, so steadily, without flaw, and she came!!!! When Karen came she let out a scream that would make a seasoned porn queen jealous, and the only sound in her ears was a echo of that scream of extacy. As she came, she felt the shadow being pumped out through her pussy after every throb. When she was done, and she laid there, sweating all over, her mouth totally dry, trying to catch her breath. She

looked at her shadow, mocking the huge wet spot she left on the sheets. Almost admiring what it had done.

As she laid there in thanks looking at the shadow, she figured out what it was. It was a perfect reflection of herself, but it was the part of herself that harbored all the feelings of never being satisfied. It was like a shell, that housed all the sexual frustration and also had her sexual dreams. She knew then, that her true happiness didn't lie within being with Craig, but within herself. Then she woke up.

She woke up breathing hard, and sweating all over her sheets. When she looked down at her sheets, between her legs, she realized she truly had a wet dream, and would have to change her sheets again. She got up to go to the bathroom to clean up, and she turned on the lamp by the door, there it was, her shadow, leaning against the opposite wall. She went to touch it, almost thinking it would touch her back, but the wall was cold, and the shadow didn't touch her back. She just kinda laughed at herself, realized Craig was no good, and felt a peace with being alone. She thought, " Well, its just me..........and my shadow".

Wicked

Pleasures™

ICE CREAM

Open up baby,
Let me in.
Let me lick your Ice Box sweetie,
Ummmm, my favorite flavor...sin.

Your body is my Neapolitan,
Three favorite flavors, I'll make my rounds.
Your tits, pussy, *and ass*,
Oh, yeah, no perversion is outta bounds.

I'll suck your nipples, like a silver spoon,
Then down to your ass when I get on a roll.
Gliding my tongue across your body like a plate,
And I'll lick that pussy to the bottom of the bowl.

You put the Ice Cream man outta business baby,
Fuck da truck, I wanna eat my lady.
Yo ass is sweetness personified in the extreme!
Consume me, Drown me, Cover me,
In your Ice Cream.

PAIN

Oh shit, my master is home,
I hear the click, click, click of my chain.
As she tightens her grip, I'm her mutha fuckin' dog,
I'm her bitch, and she feeds off my pain.

She walks across my body,
She uses my dick as her cane.
I kiss the ground that she walks on, and become the ground on which she stands.
She looks down and laughs, at my pain.

She punishes me for thinking straight!
She rewards me for going insane!
My emotions are nothing but her plaything,
She molds my yearnings,
She sculpts my pain.

My master is ready now,
I'm ready to swallow her rain.
I owe her for all that I gain,
Because she controls my pleasure,
And she owns, my PAIN.

ORGASM

The very essence that courses inside you,
Beggin' for the ultimate release.
Time to lose myself inside you,
Time for this playin' shit ta cease.

To travel down your erotic river,
Building you up to that *screaming* peak.
As I drop down on my knees to serve you,
After that pearl tongue target I seek.

Licking up and down,
Then round and round,
Like a hard, wet dick.
Teasing that pussy, rolling each lip,
Then a tongue massage on your clit.

That's right, grab my head, scream in pleasure,
As you grind on my fuckin' face!
Use my *entire* mouth as your vibrator,
I'll be your toy just to get a taste.....

Of that sweet-ass cum,
As my tongue licks deep into your hole.
Cause I'll do *anything* for your orgasm, baby,
I'll do *anything* to drink your soul.

Head

Oh shit,
Your hands slide across my pants.
From this moment on,
You got me locked in a trance.

As you pull down my draws,
And take my dick in your hand.
I know that first lick is coming soon,
The anticipation, I can't stand!

You wore that blood-red lipstick,
Baby you know just what I like.
You got skills with them lips,
Ya neva nick, scrape, or bite.

My heart skips a beat,
As I watch you glide your way down.
I think of how good it's gonna be,
I even get off on the sound!

When you swallow every inch you can,
As your mouth milks my dick.
I can hear your tongue against me,
And my dick ramming against your spit.

Then your tongue hits my spot,
And my dick jumps in your mouth!
"Suck that mutha-fuckin dick baby!"
No disrespect, but ya makin me shout!

I watch my dick slide across your lips,
It's like my eyes are on zoom!
I fell the pressure building up,
Damn, I'm gonna cum soon!!

Your pace is getting faster,
Your job is almost done.
I grab a handful of your hair,
"Dayumit Baby! HERE I CUM!!"

I give you **everything** I got,
All over your face, neck, and bed.
Damn I love you baby,
And I love the way you give me head.

THE TRIAL OF A GOD...

The origin of Cain

The Trial Of A God

The Origin of Cain

This is the story of Cain, a fallen entity of god-like power. His life has been chronicled throughout our history. Our greatest myths throughout time, are his fondest memories of what and who he once was. He was one of the most formidable, powerful, and deadly entities throughout our existence. But with great power comes great responsibility; even beings with god-like power can cross the line. Cain crossed that line, and in doing so, stood trial for his crime. This is the story of a god on trial, Ego vs. Law...with the stakes dictating the very definition of man.

On the 6th day, God created man. On the 5th day, God created the Daydreamers and Nightmares. Daydreamers, the entities that were created to satisfy the sexual needs and desires of his next creation, man. The Daydreamers are to be there at night when man and woman were to rest, to fulfill the sexual desires in our dreams, to obey every whim, complete every fantasy. The Daydreamers are there for us at night, so as they lay their heads down to sleep in the day, they leave the dreamscape, and come to our realm, the real world. Here, they roam amongst us, knowing us all intimately our most lucid fantasies. They can never be identified for each one of us sees a different person. Each mortal views a Daydreamer as his or her perfect sexual conquest.

Ladies, have you ever been out with your girls, and seen a man in a car drive by, and he was so fine that your head snapped back, and you yelled to your girls in the car, "Oh my god!!! Girl, did you see the man in that car that just went by!? He was fine as hell!!" But when you exchange notes on his appearance, your stories were different. Now you may have just excused this as a little mistake, that your girls' eyes are tripping, and you know what you saw, but you may have just seen a Daydreamer. Each one of you will see him different, each one will see what they wanted to see. This has been a common occurrence throughout history, and all through history, we have explained it away. Ever heard the phrase, "Your eyes will see what you want them to see?" Our past is clouded with common phrases that try to deflect our lack of ability to accept what we don't truly understand. It is much easier to coin a phrase, than it is to accept the fact that there are forces at work greater than our race. But for the most part, the Daydreamers are on our side. For most of us, we will only have contact with them in our dreams, where it is safe. But for the few that have contact with them in the real world, their lives will never be the same. For as perfect as the Daydreamers are for us in our dreams, they are just as deadly for us in our reality. They carry a sort of curse, a loophole of pleasure, a by-the-way of pain. For every human to have sexual contact with a Daydreamer outside the realm of the dreamscape, will have their lives change drastically for the worst. That's why the Daydreamers pick a few select humans to contact in the real world. They select the humans who have sick, perverted dreams who demoralize the dreamscape, humans who are child molesters, or murderous sex offenders. They usually make sure their punishment in the real world will fit their crimes from the dreamscape.

There are 2 Daydreamers, one male, one female.

Assante is the female, and Shoma, the male. Each is assigned to handle the entire population's dreams. Whether you are straight or gay, they will satisfy you in any way you desire in your dreams. The Daydreamers have abilities that allow them to best serve us. They can read our minds, a tool they use in the dreamscape to fulfill our fantasies, to fully and thoroughly serve us, so they know what we need to hear, what we truly want from them. They have the ability to change into other human forms, so they can be our ultimate sexual mate, conquest, or fantasy. They have the ability to feel what their sexual partner is feeling, also called a "Physical Tap"; so they can be sure all of our sensations are being fulfilled. But they do have rules they must abide by. While in our reality, they are not to perform any feats in our sight that will elude to their true nature; they are not to make themselves suspect or make us suspicious in any way. With great power, comes great responsibility. The Daydreamers do indeed have great power, but they pale in comparison to the Nightmares.

Nightmares, in the dreamscape, pull the dayshift, they handle all mortals who have sexual dreams during the day. Cain is the male Nightmare, and Fenix, the female. The power of the Nightmares are of the next level. The Nightmares have all the abilities of the Daydreamers, and then some. The Nightmares have the power to shapeshift into ANY form, human or not. They roam our reality during the night, usually causing havoc. Throughout time, we have spread stories of mythical creatures or demons that roam the earth at night. Many have been of the shapeshifting variety: vampires, werewolves, etc. All the shapeshifting creatures in our folklore have roamed the earth at night. Coincidence? NO! Very easily explained when you realize all such creatures were the Nightmares. The myth that a vampire is killed by the daylight is one example that seems to have stood the test of time. When in fact, on rare occasions, a mortal has caught a brief glimpse of a Nightmare dissipating into the dreamscape with the coming dawn. Not destroyed by the sun as the myth suggests, but with our narrow view of life, dissipation equals destruction. Roaming the earth at night, and never seen during the day, the symptom of all the great horrors in our past, and the *fingerprint* of a Nightmare. They seem to be troublemakers by nature; a side effect to one of the differences that make them what they are. You see, Daydreamers are the optimay of bisexuality. Daydreamers have no true sexual preference. But the Nightmares were able to choose their sexual orientation, and each chose heterosexual. So with the definite preference came the egos to suit. Causing havoc is something the Nightmares seem to do while experiencing mood swings. Just a way to vent, and be feared, gods with ego problems, *not* a good combination.

Nightmares also have the option to accept a mortal's dreams, or reject them. Upon rejection, they simply pull a Daydreamer into the dreamscape to fulfill the dream. A task that often times infuriates the Daydreamers, for they were probably spending their daylight hours in the real world, fulfilling their own agenda. But the Nightmares don't care. They fully know that they are the superior creation. They laugh as they watch the Daydreamers caught in the dreams they yanked them into. To the Nightmares, the Daydreamers are a joke. Cain and Fenix laugh and toy with Assante and Shoma as if they were children, meaningless pawns of no real significance. Understandably, the Daydreamers have an unyielding hatred

for the Nightmares, but have no power to enforce or act upon their yearnings for revenge. The only entity that has power over the Nightmares was the Overseer. Upon creating the Daydreamers and Nightmares, God created the Overseer to watch over and control their escapades, to step in once in a while if things ever got out of hand, and to handle with extreme prejudice, any violator of the rules. To this date, only one such occasion has arisen, only one trial has been tried, only one judgement has been rendered, and only one sentence is currently being served. Be careful, you might meet the convicted TONIGHT.

Cain, the first male Nightmare, started his carnage soon after his creation. After perusing the newly created land, he ran across a single, lovely woman. This woman seemed to be at peace, happy, content. He read her mind, and found only small traces of temptation and lust. He thought to himself, *How could this be? My very existence courses with sexuality and the primal essence of desire. Yet this woman thinks not of sex as she walks naked through this Garden of Eden. Who is this Eve? She is mortal; I can bend her will; temptation will be her undoing, lust will convict her morality, she will yearn.* So Cain assumes the shape of a snake, and we all know what happens next. I know what you're thinking, we all assume that the snake was Satan, but with all the talking the snake did, Eve never did ask him his name. In the King James version of the Bible, many things were added to the tales. Cain and Fenix shared a small conversation once on the subject, "You realize of course, that the mortals are giving all the credit for what you did against Eve, to Satan." says Fenix. Cain answered, "**Satan!!** Damn! If the mortals only knew, he ain't really worried about them, his ass neva leaves the damn house! Ok, from now on, they will know who I am. Or at least who I tell them I am. Satan's lazy ass ain't gonna get credit for my work! The mortals will know me as many different names, but they will worship me, or fear me, either way, it will be me they will pay heed to." This is the mentality of Cain, so goes the mentality of the Nightmares. Fenix, being a heterosexual female, will never follow any mortal man, only a male being of equal or greater power. She will follow Cain, she can admire and respect his power and his mind.

With the sexual orientation of a heterosexual male, Cain's ego increases over the years, decades, and centuries. As time passes, his need for mortal worshipers grows. In the earlier years, this need was smaller, he was content with his main presence being in the region of Egypt, assuming many different shapes, manifesting himself as brilliant half-human, half-animal cross breeds. Fenix too, enjoyed the rush of mortal worship, but never overstepped the rank Cain had given himself. She was content with assuming the role of your typical "Guardian"-type gods, while Cain assumed the larger roles, such as Ra, the sun god, until his need for conquest and worship mixed dangerously with his male ego: *What is the use of having such great power, if I can't truly reap the benefits? Yeah, yeah, worship, grovel, sacrifice to me, it's all getting boring. Why have the total worship of every female on the planet, and be confined to only fucking them in the dreamscape? I need more! I need to infect their real lives, not just their dreams of the day. I want them to do more than worship me, I want their lust, their yearnings, all their desires to be for me! ME! I am Cain! I am the strongest in the realm of dreams, so shall I be the strongest in the realm of reality!"*

With his mind made up, he assumed the shape of a human male. Huge in muscle mass and height, with definition never before seen, truly the greatest physical specimen on the planet. "In this realm, in this form, I shall be known as Sampson! I shall have the power of a hundred men. And with such power, I will be the most feared man by all men, and the most wanted man by all women. So says Cain, so speaks Sampson!" Cain fulfills what he has pronounced, he wreaks havoc upon the earth, claiming many lives with his strength, and many women in his bed. He feels a great sense of satisfaction, he is content for now in his current form. He becomes so content that he decides to reject all dreamers and commands Shoma, the male Daydreamer, to take his shift, fulfilling the fantasies of the mortal dreams during the day, so he may stay in the realm of reality, full-time. But what Cain doesn't realize is that his newest manifestation, and his new-found stature in the mortal world, has not gone unnoticed by the Overseer. The Overseer sees what Cain doesn't see, nor would Cain care, that the way man views himself has been drastically shattered. All over the land, mortals everywhere are speaking of Sampson, the mortal with the power of a God. Man sees a mortal form committing feats of unbelievable strength. They see a man, indestructible, unbeatable, crushing boulders in his bare hands, demolishing the walls of an enemy with a single punch, and defeating entire armies without even the use of a sword. Man's view of himself has been distorted, disfigured, and warped. Man now starts to assume that it is possible to achieve godhood for himself. There begin endless quests, with endless stories of magic elixirs, and capes of magic to achieve the power of Sampson. If one man can achieve such status and power, logic would dictate that others can. But logic deals with known factors, and Cain was an unknown entity. As man continued his fruitless pursuit of god-hood, the Overseer knew, Cain must be stopped! The progress of man must not be allowed to be tainted and twisted the way Cain was now poisoning the mind of man. It was of paramount importance that man understand his mortality, the way God created him, and live within those limitations while he progressed. The Overseer knew what he had to do, he knew that there was only one recourse available to him. There was only one hope man had to get back on track, to understand his mortality once again, one solution. Sampson must die! And he must die in a way that shows his vulnerability. The Overseer ponders shortly the best way to show man his utter and complete vulnerability. The way he dies must convey the mortality of every man, he must die in a moment that most would be vulnerable. *That's it! In the arms of a woman with whom you share your bed!* No man on the planet was to defeat Sampson. The Overseer smiled at the irony in the fact that it was to be a woman. The total irony that he was to fall because of his temptations, just like his first victim, Eve. What was that he said about Eve? "Temptation will be her undoing...", as temptation will be his.

Now, the plan was laid out, all he needed was its execution, or better yet, the executioner. He needed a woman of the dreamscape, so that she may shapeshift into a woman Cain could not resist. So he calls upon Fenix. "Fenix Nightmare, you are summoned!!" With a deep, echoing voice that seems to cover the heavens of the entire dreamscape, he has summoned the female Nightmare. A summons by the Overseer can not be ignored, whatever a being from the dreamscape is involved in, he or she will be instantly pulled out, there is no choice, there is no question, if you have been summoned, you **will** appear before him. Fenix slowly rises through the clouds that serve as a floor in the Overseer's realm. The Overseer speaks in a deep, lung-shaking voice, "Fenix Nightmare, I call upon you to handle a dire situation. Your brethren has strayed from the laws of the Nightmares. The natural progression of man is being altered as we speak. This must stop! Cain must be slain! You have been called to handle this task." Fenix ponders her situation, she knows of the Overseer's power, and aside from Cain, and God himself, the Overseer is the only being she has fear of. But Cain has been there for her since her creation. She follows him, and can not bring herself to accept what she is being commanded to do. She contemplates for a moment, *The Overseer has the power to summon me at will, and I have no choice but to appear. But if he had the power to make me follow his commands, he wouldn't be asking me to do anything, he would speak, and so it would be. Since I am not being judged here, I have committed no crime, this is not a sentence I have no decision in....it is more like a favor or request that I can refuse, and so I shall.* She addresses the Overseer, looking up into the heavens in the direction his voice bellows, "Overseer, I have committed no crime, therefore this is a request and not a judgement I am not bound to follow. I reject your request, and wish to be released from the hold of your realm. I will not turn against Cain! I will not defy him, I refuse to betray him! Now release me! Our business is done!" She feels a slight sense of fear, not knowing the reaction the Overseer will have. Does she really want to be on his bad

side? Maybe there will be a time that she will need his help. Or worse, maybe she has misunderstood the power the Overseer yields, and she might have brought a bad situation upon herself. She floats there, helpless for a short time, in perfect silence, then she feels a reaction from the Overseer. The invisible force that keeps her caged in his realm starts to tighten around her form like a python squeezing the life from its prey. As the grip gets tighter, she feels as though her existence is forfeit for her indiscretion, then, the tightening stops. The Overseer speaks. "True enough, Fenix Nightmare, you do not stand trial here and can refuse my request." The force picks her up high into a jet-black void, where she stares into total darkness, then two eyes, darker than the darkness of the void peer at her. "But know this, Nightmare, I am judge, jury, and executioner of the dreamscape. All offenses are punishable at my discretion. If you ever stand before me to be judged, mercy will escape my ears. Now go, Fenix Nightmare, be out of my realm, but never out of my sight, or my reach."

With those last words, Fenix is tossed violently back to the dreamscape. She starts to shake off the fear of the altercation she just endured. Then she thinks, and starts to smile, feeling pleased with herself. *I saved him! I saved Cain! The Overseer obviously needed me to help him. He must have needed my abilities to get close to him. Cain could never be killed by a mortal woman! Hahaha!! I did it! I can't wait to tell him!* As she gets ready to lock on to Cain's presence and go to him, she hears the Overseer call out again across the dreamscape, "Assante Daydreamer, you are summoned!" The Overseer purposely wanted Fenix to hear Assante being summoned. Normally, a summons is private, none but the required

being can hear it. So why did she hear it? What was the point? She thinks some more, *What significance could there be in letting me hear that heffa being summoned? That little piss-amt Daydreamer. They have no real power, all they can do is...* Fenix stops in mid-thought, an instant sense of terror strikes her as she finishes her thought *...all they can do is change into any human form! Oh shit! Cain! Cain is in trouble! That damn Overseer! He knew all along that he really didn't need me to do the hit on Cain. He can get that bitch-ass Daydreamer to do it! Oh shit, in Cain's current form, he will never see it coming! He's in a mortal shell, with his mortal flesh and brain, he will see Assante as all mortals do, as his perfect sexual fantasy! What did I do?? WHAT DID I DO?? I should have accepted the terms, then at least I could have betrayed the Overseer and warned Cain of his sentence. Cain doesn't even know he is being judged! I can still beat her to him! I gotta beat her to him!* Fenix instantly vanishes from the dreamscape, just a blur, a flash of light, on her way to warn Cain. She is descending upon the current location of Cain, and she doesn't see Assante or sense her presence anywhere! *I did it! I beat her here!* Then her progress is stopped suddenly as she violently hits an invisible wall of sorts. "What the hell is this??!!" She tries to fly around it, but it seems all inclusive of the surrounding territory. She yells out for Cain. "Cain!! Cain, baby you gotta hear me!!! Cain!!! YOU'RE IN DANGER!!! YOU'VE BEEN JUDGED!!! THE Daydreamer IS AFTER YOU!! TRUST NO ONE!!! **Cain, CAN YOU HEAR ME??!!!**" As she pounds on the barrier, she sees Cain can not hear a single word she is yelling to him. Fenix in now frantic, pounding away on the barrier, using every ounce of her god-like strength, but to no avail. Then she hears the bellowing voice of the Overseer. "There will be no interference with the law of the Overseer. You are now restricted from all contact with your brethren. However, Fenix Nightmare, you may watch as Cain is slain. Upon his mortal death, he will be returned to my realm, his existence is not forfeit, he will survive. But know this, Nightmare, your insolence has doomed him to a fate worse than death. Know that your outburst and refusal has forever doomed your precious one to live an existence you could never imagine. So speaks the Overseer, and so it shall come to pass!" Fenix looks up into the sky with anger in her eyes, then looks back down to the land, where she sees her loved one, Cain. She just floats there, watching him enjoy the life he has created for himself, knowing the end is near, and not being able to help him, or even warn him. She tells herself to enjoy watching Cain be Cain, one last time, one final day or so. She contemplates what fate the Overseer has in store for him, the fate worse than death. She glides her hands across the barrier, "Enjoy your last days, baby. Raise hell while you can, as only you can. I'm sorry for what I have fated you."

As she speaks those words, Assante slowly floats through the floor of the Overseer's realm. The Overseer speaks: "Assante Daydreamer, I call upon you to handle a dire situation. Cain Nightmare has strayed from the laws of the Nightmares. The natural progression of man is being altered as we speak. This must stop! Cain must be slain! You have been called upon to handle this task." Assante floats there, realizing that a summons from the Overseer, calling for the assassination of Cain is an event of monumental proportions, and after the initial shock of the request subsides, she says, "I will complete

any task you ask of me, Overseer. All I ask is that you remember my blind allegiance to your court." Immediately, a pair of soft, white eyes made of cloud formations floats down to her; the voice of the Overseer is now deep, but soft. "Assante, your allegiance has been recognized by the court, as your life is eternal, so is my gratitude. Here is your task." The story of Cain is told to Assante. Since Assante is of lower power levels and class, she was not privy to the actions throughout time of the Nightmares. After the explanation is through, she speaks to the Overseer, with a specific concern. "Overseer, Cain Nightmare will surely detect my presence as a Daydreamer. His power levels are far superior over mine. I will surely never be able to get close to him without being stricken down, much less be capable of causing his demise. I mean no disrespect to your court, but I don't know if this task you ask of me is possible. But be assured, I will die trying!" The eyes of the Overseer glow now, softly, like a warm light. "Assante, my child, you have no reason to fear. I have taken into consideration your minute power levels compared to that of the Nightmare. In his current human form, Cain has the mind of a normal human male. His mind is susceptible to your shapeshifting talents. He will see you as his perfect sexual partner. He will not be able to resist you, as no mortal can. He will accept you into his bed. And there, you will kill him." Assante speaks of another concern, "Overseer, it eases my mind to know he will accept me, but what of the fact that he has rendered himself invulnerable? What form of weapon will I yield to pierce his skin? The strongest of steel will shatter upon contact with his forged body. He has rendered himself invincible. And what's to stop him from detecting the fact that although beautiful, I am not

human? I am still a Daydreamer." The Overseer seems a little tickled by her worries, but eases them nonetheless. "Assante, do not worry, you will not be detected by the Nightmare. Nothing concerning the dreamscape entities is beyond my power. With but a thought, Cain would cease to exist. With a blink of an eye, his chiseled torso can be spread across the oceans of the earth. I will shield you from his detection. You have no worries. Here, these scissors will be your weapon. His current physical form can overpower even your greatly enhanced strength. This is where you must use your mind, Daydreamer. This is where you must be cunning. His hair is the power stem for his Nightmare essence. The shorter you cut it, the weaker he shall be. These scissors will melt right through his locks without effort. Then use the same scissors to destroy the human form he has molded. Understand me, Daydreamer, the murder of Cain must be brutal. The mortals must see this "Sampson" as more mortal than they will ever want to be. The tales of his death must be so gruesome that they will spread across all the lands. I will have other dreamscape beings replay the image in their minds, so they will never forget, that no man, may achieve god-hood." Assante does not hesitate in answering the Overseer. "I will be your assassin, Overseer, the deed shall be done." The scissors are floating in front of her. She takes them in her hand. As she gets ready to depart, she stops. "Overseer, if I may ask one last question." He answers,"You may." She thinks of how to word it, then speaks: "With your infinite control over the dreamscape entities, why did you ask me to fulfill the task? Why not just carry out the task yourself? Assuredly, it would have been less bothersome to achieve the desired result." The Overseer responds. "Sometimes it's not

the destination that's important, child, but instead, it's the long walk you take to get there, that holds the true meaning. Now go, Assante, go stop the Nightmare from contaminating the progress of man any further." And with the assassin on her way, the Overseer does was he does best, sits back and watches.

Back in the real realm, Cain is quickly achieving a king's status. He has the story tellers writing tales of his great strength and accomplishments. He is making sure that all know of his power, sending messengers to all lands. He actually sends body parts from fallen enemies with the messengers to make sure the tales of his exploits are taken as fact, that he is the most powerful man on the planet!

That night, Cain feels a sense of accomplishment. He has fed his ego, now it was time to feed his sexuality. He retires to his harem of women, a legendary cast of the most beautiful women in the land. The stories of his sexual exploits are as popular as his moments on the battlefield. Cain, not being a true human, the fact that he is a pure sexual being, has a well-deserved reputation amongst all women that have fallen victim to his sexual needs. He has no sexual limits; a hunger never satisfied. The screams can be heard all night, every night, non stop. Woman after woman tries to totally satisfy him, and each fail, walk out of his temple, holding their guts, not believing that all the rumors were true, until now.

But as Cain was proud of his reputation in battle, he was equally as proud of his sexual reputation, knowing that no woman could handle him, ever. To be known all across the planet as the strongest man, with the biggest muscles, and the biggest dick! Now that was a reputation! "No man can slay

me, no woman can handle me!" That was a commonly heard phrase as he sat around with his followers, eating and drinking, being loud and barbaric. Then one day, a young messenger came running into his place with stories of a woman with beauty, never before seen. A woman beyond comparison, and without equal. Immediately Cain orders all messengers to get word to this woman. "I want her! The greatest male on the planet, must have the best female! Who is this Delilah? Bring her to me!"

Days go by, then weeks. Cain spends each night now, alone, not having anything to do with any woman that approaches him, for his palate only longs for one. "Why can't anyone find her?! What's the problem?" He summons his private squire, "Carry this message to all. If the woman, Delilah, is not found by the week's end, all who have failed in their mission to find her, shall die! So speaks Sampson!"

This sends all trackers on a frenzy, fearing desperately for their lives, asking all who claim to have seen her, for the most detailed descriptions possible, so artists can render a likeness for them to go by. But everyone who swears to have seen this woman of unparalleled beauty, has a different story of her appearance. Soon, the trackers give up hope. Not one likeness, from any witness, matches any other. It's the 6th day, and Cain announces that tomorrow, is their last day.

That night, as Cain lie in bed thinking of this woman of whom he now yearned for, he is visited. His bedroom door cracks open, the light from the hall candles pierces the lonely darkness of his room. There, in the small blade of light, stands Delilah, aka Assante. As she stands there, she is 6 feet tall with the body of a warrior. Strong, muscular legs; toned, defined

arms, but still very feminine. The perfect combination of grace, beauty, and power. Her facial features are very exotic. Long, Asian-type eyes that are cold and calculating, but very seductive. A petite nose that almost seems to disappear when Sampson is distracted by her flawless lips. Lips that are not too thick, with perfect form, as though they were painted by the world's finest artists on their best day. Her skin was a smooth, milky, caramel brown. So smooth, Sampson thought his hands would sink into her flesh if he touched her, as though her skin flowed over her body like the ocean caresses the earth. Delilah was indeed all the rumors said she was. But the exterior was merely a decoy. As a ninja wears black, Assante wears beauty.

Sampson lights some candles so that he may view her in better light. With each lighting of a candle, as the room became more and more illuminated, Assante's beauty seemed to multiply. There was now a warm, romantic glow about the room, and still, she stands by the door, not moving, not saying a word, just watching him, studying him, realizing that in a few moments, she must butcher his perfect body. As Cain lights the last candle, he walks back to his bed and lies down. Turning on his side, he slides over to give her room to get into his bed. Sampson speaks. "Approach me, Delilah, I have waited for this moment far too long. Come to your king, come share my bed." Normally, King Sampson would not have to speak to any female to achieve sexual favors, but the mere beauty of this woman demanded even his ultimate respect. But even so, he did not expect her response. "I have traveled many miles to rendezvous with you, my lord, can you not dismount your bed, and walk the very few steps to meet me? I offer no resistance," she said as she held out her arms as though she is yearning for him. "Come, my lord, come conquer me, as you have the world."

Sampson had never before in his life had to go to a woman, he always made them approach him. But for some reason, the demeanor of Delilah was irresistible to him. Her beauty commanded respect, and her will enforced it. So for the first time in his life, he does as a woman told him to do. He slides out of his bed, and slowly walks to her. He is wearing a black toga, with a solid gold belt. He stands a solid 8 feet tall, with no trace of body fat. His skin is very dark, almost as dark as his intense eyes. Every step he takes, shows the definition, the rippling of his muscles, the raw, pure power he yields. She swears she can feel the ground shake as he approaches her, and she looks at his arms and legs, the way the muscle looks as though it is in combat with his skin, as if in any second the skin will give way to his power and not be able to hold this massive man's bulk and strength. But she keeps her cool. She has the scissors in a pouch looped over the sash holding her dress. Her dress is white, and almost see through. It's a linen-type material, seemingly very light, but heavy to the touch, a very durable garment for the conditions she supposedly had traveled. Sampson has now reached her, and is just staring at her face, then into her eyes.

"I have found my Queen," Sampson speaks as he gently cups her face in his massive hands. She gazes into his eyes and sees his gratification, like a long-sought journey is finally over. Little does he know, that it is more than just his search for a perfect beauty that has come to an end this night, but so will his existence as a Nightmare, providing she can fulfill her end of the contract. She is starting to have serious doubts in her mind, thinking the weapon the Overseer armed her with is not sufficient for the job. Afterall, the scissors were not that big, only having a 6-inch blade. And in looking at the massive frame of Cain as Sampson, surely she could not dismantle such a body with such a small weapon, much less even hope to kill him, for that matter. But the Overseer told her that the scissors would do the job just fine, and so she trusted him. The worst thing that could happen is that she could suffer a mortal death, have to put up with the short agony of having her limbs ripped from her body, but all would be right afterwards and she would be able to keep the good graces of the Overseer for her efforts. But as she thought over the situation, she felt Cain go for her bag. *Oh no, I'm caught, she thought. I'm dead for sure!* She quickly snaps out of her thought, and reaches down for her bag, grabbing Sampson's hand. "Careful, my lord. Please, this is all I have left of my dear grandmother. She left me this before she passed."

"Not to fear, my queen, I am only attempting to disrobe you, so that I may personally cleanse your body after your long journey to me. From this moment on, you will be treated as my queen. Bathdrawers! Run a bath for your new queen! Use only the freshest roses, or you will lose one finger or toe for every wilted petal in her bath! Now go, and be quick about it!" Quickly, a huge pot was lifted off of a massive fire. A long, thick wooden pole had a rope tied around it and was attached to the pot. It took 12 strong men to transport it and deliver the hot, steamy water, into the deep, gold and black marble bath-tub. The tub was huge, to accommodate Sampson's size. 10-feet long, 7-feet wide, and 3-feet deep, a small pool. The petal bearers carefully and quickly sorted the rose petals, and placed

a total of 5 dozen roses in her bath. Bathing oils were added to make sure her skin maintained its moisture. All in all, the team had her bath ready and waiting in 5 minutes. A member of the team notified Sampson. "Sire, her bath is ready." Immediately, Sampson's nose flares, his eyes lock in on the messenger, and he swoops down upon him, grabbing his entire head with one hand and lifting him off the floor to his eye level. "Her!!?? You dare address your queen as HER!?? You do not deserve to live long enough to even suffer for your insolence!" As those words are spoken, Sampson starts to squeeze the head of the messenger, as the messenger screams in pain. Assante interrupts, "My king, if I may, please spare him for now, if for no other reason, so that you will not soil your hands before my bath. I don't want the blood of a messenger in my bath water. That is my right as your queen, is it not?" She is very careful at how she has phrased her words, she knows that she cannot challenge him by directly telling him to stop, that would only make things worse, if that were even possible. She had to find a way to save the messenger's life, for in the messenger's dreams, he was always good to her, and this was her way of giving back to him. So, with a small sarcastic smile, she asks the question that in hopes, will save the young man's life from the angry Nightmare. Instantly, Sampson drops the messenger and the messenger runs off, staggering, holding his head in great agony, but alive. Sampson laughs. "Delilah, you will surely make a fine queen, with such wits about you to compliment your beauty. You will make a fine queen, indeed. Come, my queen, let us purify your body in my bath."

"As you wish, my king," Assante replied. With that being said, Sampson sweeps her off her feet, and carries her to the bathing quarters. Alone, with the smell of roses mixing with hot steam rising from the massive tub, he undresses her. Slowly, he unwraps her cloth belt, taking her guarded pouch carefully in his hands and placing it on a marble block next to the tub. She watched pensively as he handled the pouch, just waiting for him to look in it. The tension was killing her, but he didn't look in the pouch. To him, it was insignificant, he would handle it with care as asked by his new queen, but the prize he wanted, stood before him.

As he began to disrobe her, he watched how her hair fell against her neck. Black flowing locks, seemingly splashing against her delicate neck like waves crashing into a cliffside. Her shoulders were strong, yet delicate. Her whole body was toned and in perfect shape. Her breasts were the size of his huge hands, and she had a round, thick ass to match. Her stomach was well defined with a gold hipchain that draped itself around her, and hung down to the start of her trimmed pubic hair. Oh, he was gonna love this, after all the women that have come in and out of his bed, he finally had one he wanted to savor. He did not want to rush this experience, but take it in slowly, as you would drink fine wine.

When she was completely nude, he picked her up, cradled her in his arms, and slowly lowered her into the massive bathtub. As he lowered her into the water, he watched how the water seemed to consume her body, as if the water itself was hungry for her beauty. He lowered her very slowly, taking at least a full minute or two just to get her all the way in. As she lay there, secure in his giant, powerful arms, she went limp, and let him handle her. She knew she was safe with him, he was the strongest man on the planet, and his grip, and arms

felt like hot, tempered steel. So she relaxed, totally, and felt the water slowly swallow her. She loved the sensation of the cool air on her upper body, in direct contrast to the hot steam rising up from the bath, making her backside sweat from the heat. All the while, she was being lowered so slowly, the water seemed to be coming up to her, not her coming to it. Her toes entered first as she was being lowered in a full-lying-down position. The hot water stung her toes, but no other part of her body. The anticipation of how it would feel when it slowly crept to her private areas was killing her, but she was thoroughly enjoying her wait. Seductively, the water crept up her body, from her toes, then as her legs felt the heat, so did her ass. "Ooooohhh," she let out a long, soft, whisper of pleasure. The rate of descent is so slow, that her ass is wet for a good 20 seconds before any part of her back touches the water. Up the water crept, finally touching her back, and now her vaginal area. Hot water, filling every pore of her body, making its way to her clit. Then it hits her, the water seemingly swallows her clit, like the bathtub opened its warm lips, and took her into its mouth. The hot rose-scented water totally relaxed her, as now the water was wrapping its wet arms and legs around her body, sliding around her waist, filling her navel, and working towards her breasts. Almost completely submerged, the water was sliding up into her cleavage, wrapping itself around the base of her breasts like pythons. Her nipples were rock hard as the hot water made the air on her nipples seem like freezing arctic wind in comparison. Slowly she was lowered. She couldn't wait for the water to get to her nipples. Up and up the water came, as she breathed harder and harder with each inch she was lowered. Then, like a sinking ship that lost its battle with the ocean, the hot bath, made for a queen, consumed her nipples in one quick, tingling motion. She let out a small sigh of relief, then, Cain let her sit on one of the sitting blocks in the tub. She is incredibly turned on. She has not experienced this form of foreplay before. She's like a kid in a candy store. There are many firsts for her this night. This is the first time she has walked the earth at night, and seen a real human evening. She is in the midst of being seduced by the sole, one and only male Nightmare, and she knows sex is soon to follow. The excitement is almost too much, but she tells herself to enjoy the moment, and keeps reminding herself that she must soon kill this man

Slowly, he washes every inch of her body with his strong, steel grip, massaging her legs, her back, and her breasts in the hot, perfumed water. She looks into the water as he washes her, his strong forearms caressing her and caring for her. At this moment she can't help but wonder what this man could have done to deserve execution. But she knows it's not her place to question the decision of the Overseer. An arrow never questions the bow from which it was launched, it just stays true to its course, and strikes where aimed. And the Overseer had aimed her at Cain.

When her bath was completed, Cain picked her up and carried her into the bedroom area.
As she lay in his arms, she could feel the ground shake under his massive body with each strong, sure step. His unbridled power was euphoric in nature, as she was seemingly drunk with anticipation. Step after step, the earth itself seemed to give way to his strength, almost caving in underneath his body. But his stride was deliberate, the boudoir was their destination. He

would have her, and he would have her soon.

Finally, they approach the bedroom. With no effort, he adjusts her body in one of his arms as if he were cradling a little baby, lengthwise, with her back lying across the length of his forearms, his hand on her ass, and her head lying against his shoulder. Then, with his free hand, he opens the door, and proceeds to light the room candles. He holds her as if she were weightless, but with all the untold power he commands, he is extremely gentle with her. As he proceeds to prepare the room for their night, he holds her still, every movement is smooth, careful not to disrupt her. He was so careful, she could have easily fallen asleep in his one arm, and never been at risk of being awakened by any sudden movements. He had total control of the situation, and her body. Then, as the last candle was lit, he laid her down on the bed.

After the hot bath, and being held in Cain's hard, hot arms, the cool hand-woven silk sheets welcomed her naked body. There she lay as she watched Cain walk to the other side of the room to disrobe. He takes his toga off and lies it in a pile with identical clothes of its type. And there he stands, 8 feet of god-like man. Pure muscle, flawless dark brown skin, and perfectly sculpted. She just watched in amazement; even in the dreamscape, of all the millions of dreams she has fulfilled, none, not one man, has come close to even dreaming himself to be such a perfect symbol of domination. Then he turned to her and walked towards her, slowly across the room as though stalking her. A huge, dark mass hunting her, like a dark, stormy cloud on approach to strike down upon her with all its might. She could see him getting closer and closer, with each step, it seemed as though he grew another foot in height. But

she knew it was the excitement of the moment playing tricks with her mind. As Cain was now only about 6 or 7 feet away from her, she could see in full view all his dimensions, and he was huge! She knew she had to adjust her insides so she could handle him. This was always the tricky part of her job. While on earth, she had to adjust to accommodate her body to fit the size of the man before actual penetration. To make adjustments later would cause serious suspicion amongst mortals, but to do so with a Nightmare, a fellow occupant of the dreamscape, would be a sure-fire and deadly give away. So she had to make her adjustments, and make them fast. Cain, as Sampson took joy in punishing the mortal women, so he was hung like a horse. Even limp, he was a strong 11 inches, so she had to calculate how he would be fully erect. She figures she better give herself 15 inches at least, then figures that no mortal woman is going to be deeper than that. But she knew he could grow past that, and this was gonna hurt! But she had a job to, and this was the one night she was granted to complete it. "Come to me, my king, come claim what you have rightfully earned for all your battles. Fill me with your power, share with me your strength. My body is but an empty vase until filled with the man that I shall know till death do us part." Her words are sure and soft. Cain, for once in his life, lets his guard down. The combination of Delilah's physical beauty, and her calming, welcoming voice, has extinguished the anger that normally fuels the destructive fires in his heart. No, for once he will know peace. For once he will share his bed, in the true sense of the word **share**. They will be as one. His search for a queen is over, it's time to settle down and enjoy the first night of what he sees as many. "Till death do us part, my queen, yes,

finally, till death do us part." He doesn't know how true his words ring. That he will measure his days with his queen not by the decade, not by the years, but by the hours, and by the minutes. His time with his new beloved shall not be understood by the calendar, but by the sundial. With those words being said, he slides into the bed next to Delilah, takes her in his arms, and pulls her on top of him as they share a long, passionate kiss. As their tongues touch, Assante inadvertently, and probably out of pure instinct, tries to do a physical tap to fully enjoy the sensation. As the thought hits her mind to do it, a same thought warns her against it. If she uses any of her dreamscape abilities while in contact with the Nightmare, he would surely be alerted. She was not sure of the extent of camouflage the Overseer has granted her. She knew that physically, he could not see though her guise, but his mind might be a different story, and the true power of dreamscape entities comes into play during physical contact. So, to be sure, from here on out, she was to finish the episode as a mortal, a handicap for sure, but viewing herself as a superior being than mere mortal females. She figures if they can do it, she can do it. Now, the game was afoot, the board had been set, all the players were in place, and with Cain in the bed, the dice have been rolled.

The task is at hand. Cain pulls her onto his enormous, perfect frame. They kiss softly at first, gentle, loving. His hands glide up and down her back. Tracing her spine, then massaging her, off and on, running his fingers through her long locks of hair, then back down her back again. He carefully makes his strokes longer and longer, closer and closer to her round, firm ass. Over and over, throughout their first stage of intimacy, he speaks the phrase, "Till death do us part, till death do us part, my love," whispering the words gently, affectionately. To him, these are words of relief, a quest completed, a love finally found. To her, they are a haunting reminder of the deed to come. Like a free fall from a cliff, tranquil, soft, quiet, until the harsh reality of ground zero ends your flight. She saw this time with Cain as the peaceful flight they would share together, but his words "till death do us part" were just a reminder that the Overseer's sentence was the ground zero rushing up their way, to end their one night of ecstasy. As she ponders her inevitable situation, she is snapped out of her thought by the feeling of Cain's finger moving in circles, slowly, lightly, across her vaginal area. Now she was back into it. She figures *if you know you're gonna hit bottom anyway, why not enjoy the fun of the fall.* The pace of the session was picking up, becoming more physical, more intense. Cain slowly massages her clit as he kisses her lips softly, then slides down towards her body. She looks down at him as she feels his tongue rolling down her cleavage, towards her right breast as he holds it firmly in his hands. All she can really see is his massive back, rippling shoulders holding his body up so he would not crush her. One arm easily supporting all his weight over the top of her body, as the other hand was busy caressing her now wet lips. She can now feel her nipple rise into his mouth as he is rolling his tongue around, gently pressing her nipple against the roof of his mouth with his tongue. A soft, wet, warm, flesh sandwich, for her sensitive nipples and breasts. "Ummm, yes my king, yes, I am yours, do with me what you may." Assante knows how to cater to a man's ego, after all, it is in her genetic makeup. Her sole creation revolves

around satisfaction, but without the use of the psychic abilities, she will have to depend upon past experiences, and assume she is saying what he wants to hear. Then, immediately after those words are spoken, Cain stops. All licking, sucking, and touching suddenly stops. He pulls his hand from between her legs, and supports himself with two hands, laying directly over her, looking down into her eyes, very intensely. She is now scared. *What did she do? What did she say wrong? What is he going to do to her?* Worse yet, the scissors are still in the washroom. The only weapon in existence that can penetrate his flesh, is a good 50 yards away. She is in a most vulnerable position. Although she is a Daydreamer, a magical being of great strength, agility and power, Cain is a Nightmare. His power is easily 100 fold over hers. He is the male of the dominant creation, the strongest of the strong. And now, for some reason, he has stopped, and is staring her down. For what seems an eternity to her, he just hovers over her, staring into her eyes. She can see that he is contemplating something, but what? *Is he merely thinking about what to do next? Is he admiring her beauty? Or did the Overseer betray her for unknown reason? Did Fenix make a deal with the Overseer? Is her camouflage broken?* For all she knows, at this very moment, Cain sees her for what she truly is, and he is thinking of the best way to tear her limbs from her body, and make her suffer. She can hear her breath growing shallow with fear. She starts to slide back, to at least come from underneath his body. As she starts to squirm back, Cain puts his massive hand around her waist. One steel grip, totally wrapped around the front of her midsection, his thumb is on one side of her waist, and his fingers wrap around the other. Now she is stuck, and

his expression hasn't changed, not even a blink. She can't take it anymore, she has to find out what's going on, she knows something is wrong, so she figures she will take the offensive. Maybe she can focus all of her strength into one blow, catching him off guard enough for her to run and get her weapon. She knows that under normal circumstances, a blow from her, no matter the force, would not have enough force to knock water off his back. But right now, he wasn't expecting it, or so she thought. With that in mind, she builds up her internal energies, like a human will focus a blow to one singular point, so shall she. She concentrates, never taking her eyes off of his, not wanting to give him warning. She's ready to strike, when suddenly he speaks, breaking her concentration. "I have truly never been bewitched by a woman's beauty, until now. Every second I gaze upon your beauty, it is like looking into the most beautiful of oceans. I always see a glimmer of perfection I didn't notice the moment before. Do not move, just relax. I have never tasted the nectar of a woman, and now, I shall. You shall be my nectar of victory. My war against my inner demons has been won. I shall use the vessel you have pledged to me as a goblet. I shall drink deep, making our bodies as one. I shall carry you in my blood from this moment on, my love. Anything you ask of me, I shall do." For what seemed an eternity to her, was in truth only a few moments as he gazed at her. There was no intention to hurt her, only admire. She realized that she had best be careful, she had relied too much in the past on the psychic ability to know what a man was thinking. She had best not make a mistake and overreact again. Relieved that all was good, she tries to relax. She knows that relaxing will become a whole lot easier soon, as the Nightmare is now licking the

inside of her thighs.

Assante takes a deep breath, then lets it out, relaxing, and letting her body once again go limp in Cain's arms. Cain said he has never tasted a woman before, but that doesn't mean he doesn't know what he's doing. She is fully aware, and excited because she knows that like her, he is a sexual entity. He knows all points of pleasure, and all that fuels desire. When a fish is born to water, it will swim right away, no practice necessary, that is what comes natural. And now, Cain is about to get his tongue wet for the first time.

He licks all around her inner thighs. His tongue is strong, like a soft, hot, smooth, hand rubbing her thighs down. She can feel the muscles in her thighs melt like butter into his mouth. Round and round his tongue rubs her down. It feels as though his sexy, full lips are swallowing her silky skin as he advances upward. Soon, very soon, those lips will be licking her lips, deep, long, soft, and wet. The anticipation was killing her, but she knew that he was in full control of the situation, and knew fully knew what he was doing. Before any part of what he was doing became boring for her, he would move to the next spot. Like he knew for certain the threshold of pleasure for each location. Now, he was sliding up the hairline of her pubic hair. Tracing in circles, rolling his tongue slowly across its outline. It tickled a bit, but more than that it made her muscles jump. He had her twitching like a virgin, and she loved it. She kept her eyes closed, relaxing fully, to mentally take in the entire gambit of sensations. Then she felt his breath against her lips. Hot, steamy, seductive air, so close she knew his lips had to be closer than one could measure. She waited eagerly, clenching her eyes tighter, waiting for that first contact, that first lick, anything! But for now, all she felt was that hot, intense air, his lips waiting for that perfect moment to touch her. Just the anticipation had her heart racing, her breath was getting faster, her back was starting to arch, trying to casually force a little contact. But to no avail, she had to wait, he bid his time, letting her build up, then, when she was ready to just slide down and pounce onto his lips, CONTACT!

The first contact was a soft, gentile kiss. Right on her lips, and then, slow, wet, deliberate kisses, up her valley, towards her clit. Each kiss had a sucking motion, pulling a small portion of her lips into his mouth. Kiss after kiss, he moved up, slow, about 10 seconds passing before the next contact. It got to where she could anticipate contact before it happened, and she would take a deep breath right before he touched her, bracing herself for the erotic blow. Now, he had worked his way up, and she knew the next kiss was the one, the next kiss would hit her directly, squarely, exactly on her spot, and she could barely breathe, she was so excited. She felt she was going to die any second if he didn't touch her soon, but he let her shake an extra 5 seconds this time, until he saw her making a tight fist, clenching in anticipation. Then, finally, he gave her what she was waiting for, and he gave it to her good. She had her eyes closed, waiting for that contact, and then she felt him, his lips consuming her clit, catching her totally off guard. Not the small kiss she was anticipating, but a full, wrap around, out-right consumption. The most sensitive part of her body was now cut off from the outside world and in his mouth.

Like two lovers rolling around on top of each other, he was rolling her clit around in his mouth. She could feel her energies building up as she felt her clit glide across the entire

length of his tongue. He took his time, he rolled the underside of his tongue across her so she could feel its perfect smoothness, how soft it felt next to her, then back to the front, the caressing pressure he was putting against her. He was building her up perfectly, starting a even pace, licking her up and down, staying focused on her spot. Incredibly simplistic and effective, staying on target, with more and more pressure, sucking her harder and harder, slowly, but steadily. He never stopped his pace, he never had a break in his pattern, she was able to totally relax without worry of a break in the action. This was going to be perfect! She felt herself building up to cum, she felt the raw energy within her, like the flow of electricity waiting to be released, her thighs were shaking, and just as she felt as though she wanted to start bucking on his face, he grabbed her hand placed it firmly on the back on his head. He was letting her know that he felt the aggressiveness inside her, and it was okay to let it out. That was the one thing missing, and now she was able to exert all the energy she felt building up. She grabbed the back of his head, hard, and started bucking into his lips. He stayed true to form, never leaving her spot. A perfect lock, no matter what she did, he was going to keep on pleasing her. She could totally let loose, and she did. She arched her back and was now literally fucking his face, throwing herself into his mouth, and he took it all with no problem. He was perfect in every way, unselfish, and extremely skilled, almost too perfect, for he knew her body as well as she did. And now she was ready to let it all out. A true mortal orgasm, not reached by magical means, or ordered by command in the dreamscape, but built slowly, steadily, without a hitch, without flaw, and now was the payoff. "Ohhh, yes!! YES,

SAMPSON!! YES!!!" She put both hands on the back of his head, and sat up, pushing herself into his face as hard as she could. Screaming, almost growling, she cums, and Sampson takes all she can give him. He wraps his hands around her waist and does what he had proclaimed he would do, literally picked her up off the bed, he held her as he would a goblet, and drank the nectar of his queen. She could feel his lips move against her lips as he swallowed, over and over again. Holding her shaking body still, secure, until she came so hard, she had nothing left. Her body went limp, as she collapsed back towards the bed, her head being the only part of her body to actually hit the pillows because he was still holding her up, licking what he could off her lips. Finally, as she jumped while he licked off all he could, he looked down and saw that for all the power he had at his disposal, he yielded to her. He let her express herself while he held his ego in check. As she contemplated the "whys" of the current situation, Cain quickly answered it for her; for now he was sliding on top of her, and he was rock hard. He had let her have her moment, so now it was time for him to exert himself. He had let a woman be a woman, now, it was time for a man to be a man. And in Assante's mind, after the extreme pleasure he had given her, it was a fair trade. "I drank from your sweet glass, my queen, swallowed your cherished nectar, now, let's see what's at the bottom of that glass shall we?"

Quickly, Assante looked down so she could see what she had to deal with, but it was too late. He was in her, and he was very forceful. She made herself 15 inches in depth, and quickly learned that she didn't give enough. Cain wasn't human, but he gave his human form incredible proportions.

She was out of breath, out of energy, and totally exhausted from her experience. But now, she had to contend with him. What was she gonna do? She made herself as close to mortal as a Daydreamer can, to best conceal her identity. But now, how was she going to handle him? As that thought crossed her mind, she felt a jolting pain. It was Cain, digging deep into her insides. He seemed pleased that he was able to enter so far without hurting her up until now. "You are so perfect for me, it's as though you were made just for me, only for me, And I, for you." He had now found the limit she could handle, so he eased off, so she could enjoy him. He knew just how much to give her; he knew a little pain here and there was good. She could feel his incredibly long strokes, sliding in and out of her. His god-like body, there to make love to her, along with a keen sense of what she needed and wanted. He knew that she was tired, and that was going to be what made it exciting for her. And again, he was right.

Assante could feel his strokes getting harder and longer. They had both worked up a good sweat after 30 minutes of steady strokes. Now, he was in his stride, constantly hitting her back walls with each thrust. His stamina was amazing as he pulled back almost all the way for each stroke. She felt him, every inch slide all the way back, 15 inches back, then 15 inches in. Over and over and over he came at her harder and harder. He was fucking the air out of her lungs. He felt so deep, that every full thrust pushed the air right out of her body. She had to time her breath, inhale while he pulls out, exhale when he thrusts. It was a job to handle him, but with the pain, came great pleasure. She kept wanting to quit, she was so tired, but she felt she had to keep going. She felt like she had to stop, every 10 minutes she thought she was going to pass out, that she couldn't handle anymore, but she would just claw into those tremendous muscles on his back and hold on. She would beat on his chest to try to expend or dissipate in some-way, the force he was putting into her, but that just made him thrust all the harder. She would feel her orgasms build up harder and harder, coming at regular intervals, as though her body was greedy and pleasing itself until nothing was going to be left to survive on. She came so many times, it started to hurt to cum again. She tried to slide back a little to get a small break, but then he reached back, took both of her legs, wrapped them around him, and walked her to the wall. She thought he was going to ease up because he was pretty gentle with her as they walked across the room, but he never exited her. He was being careful not to hit her too hard against the stone walls. Then, once against the wall, he was right back at it, fucking her standing up, and all she could do was hold on and take it. She wished she could use the abilities to read his mind, find out what it was going to take to make him stop, but she knew he would stop when he was ready, he would cum when he felt like it. Minutes passed, each minute making the next minute another challenge, until an hour passed, and she felt like she was going to finally pass out. Was she going to be sent back to the Overseer, fucked to death? "Please cum, my king, please, please cum for me." Right after she speaks those words, she feels Cain's pace reach blistering speeds, and she knows he's ready. She thinks, *That's all I had to do? All I had to do was ask? I took this beating for all these hours, and PLEASE was the dayum key?! What kind of sense did that make??!!* Then she remembered his words as he gazed upon her before this all started, “Anything you ask of me, I shall do.” And so he did. She figured she’d really test it, she wanted it over, and she wanted, needed, it to stop now! “Come for me, NOW! COME IN ME, NOW!!!!!” Immediately after her words are spoken, Cain literally sinks his fingers into the solid stone walls, and roars like the king of the beasts as she feels his mortal-like cum fill her body. It is a soothing warmth, slick and electric. He holds her still the whole time, but she can feel him jumping inside of her, a muscular, powerful pump, giving her the reward she worked so hard for.

Now, it was time for bed. “Carry me, my lord. Carry me for I am too tired to walk.” “Anything you ask of me, my queen. Till death do us part.” Finally he exits her, and she feels as though she gave birth. A huge weight is off of her body, but she still has his prize coursing inside of her. It’s a gratifying feeling. He carries her back to the bed and tucks her in. After a long kiss goodnight, they both fall fast to sleep. As she drifts off, she awakens in the dreamscape, in the Overseer’s realm. Once again, the eyes of the Overseer cut through the darkness, and are peering at her. “Assante Daydreamer, you have almost completed your task. You have done well, my child. You have seduced the stray Nightmare. Now go, finish your assignment, so that I may bring him to justice.” The Overseer’s voice seems pleased, like he was eagerly anticipating Cain’s arrival in his realm following his death at Assante’s hands. But all Assante can remember is her time with the Nightmare. All the pleasure he gave her, and how perfect he was. She had to know the full story of Cain’s crimes. What did he really do to deserve such a fate? “Overseer, may I ask why....” her question is cut short as the eyes darken in anger,

and quickly approach her. He speaks, this time, in a calm, yet aggravated tone, "Little one, I give you this chance to think twice and not question this court. I see you very favorably, thus I warn you against the grave mistake you would make so easily. Now think for a moment on the importance of your questioning me, as well as the importance of your comfort in your eternal existence. Eternity is a long time to spend in.......discomfort." As she thinks, the eyes of the Overseer circle her, constantly, quiet, no noise or wind, no pupils, just darkness, empty darkness. "I understand, Overseer, and accept my gratitude for the chance you have given to avoid your wrath. I will do as you have asked of me. May I be released so I may make this as quick as possible, and return to you your stray Nightmare." Her words hurt to utter, but she knows that she cannot save Cain, and her very existence was in jeopardy now; she had to do what she agreed to do. A deal is a deal, even in the dreamscape. Now the eyes of the Overseer lighten, soft pupils come in, and the tone of his voice is very light. "You have chosen well, little one, in your decision, and your words. Yes, go now, and know that you have pleased me on this day." With that said, she drops though the clouds that make the floor of the realm, and wakes up in the room, next to Cain. She knows what she must do, and she knows that she must do it fast. The sun will rise soon, and he must be dead by morning so that all will see his vulnerability, as commanded by the Overseer. She looks at Cain, lying there asleep. She knows that this is the closest she will ever come to finding a true mate. She will never again know what it is like to share a bed with a dominant, more powerful male. Once Cain is dead, there will be no male entity of greater power than she. Shoma, the male

Daydreamer is a dreamscape entity, true enough. But he is of equal strength and power. Not like Cain; she liked the power Cain wielded. There was one male she could call dominant, she had one night with him, and now, there would be none. For one night, she found her king, and in one moment, she shall claim another victim. He thinks he has found his queen, when in truth, what he has found is his executioner. Assante, the assassin.

There she lie, next to him. Now was the time to do her deed before he could wake up. She quietly rolls off the bed to retrieve her pouch, and remembers she has a long walk to the washroom. Slowly, quietly, she sneaks across the room. She is careful to step lightly, gently putting her weight down on each step; long, careful strides to get her from the bed to the door, quickly and efficiently. Soon, she reaches the door, and cracks it open. Luckily, Cain is very meticulous about the details of his palace, so the doors make no noise when opened. Thus, her departure goes unnoticed. Soon, she is nearing the washroom area, and she is nervous because she knows her time is running thin. She has a brisk walk now, jogging occasionally. Finally, she enters the washroom, lights the room candles, and runs to the marble stand where Cain put her pouch down. *Oh No!! IT'S NOT HERE!!! IT'S GONE!!! DAMMIT!!!* She scurries over to the entrance and lights some candles so she may search with some light. *Maybe it fell down.* She's nervous, down-right scared, and she's searching, frantically. She's rubbing her hands across the floor, searching on her hands and knees, and talking to herself. "I'M DEAD! If I don't find those scissors, I'M DEAD! I HAVE TO HURRY UP AND GET BACK BEFORE HE WAKES UP! Why did I agree to

this...WHY??!!" Just as she is contemplating what will happen if Cain wakes up and catches her missing, she hears the door open up behind her. She's on all fours right now, with her back turned to the door. She knows it's Cain, she doesn't know what to say to him to explain her position, and why she snuck out of his bed. She's ready for the worst, she knows it's over, and she turns slowly to face him. As she looks up to explain to her king, she sees it's not him.

It's not Cain, but the servant she saved from Cain earlier. He was bruised and beaten, standing there in the light of the doorway, staring at her. For a moment, their eyes lock, as she wonders why he is there, and he is shocked to see the new queen in such a laboring position. Then, he carefully closes the door behind him, and approaches her with his hand out. *HE HAS MY POUCH!* He speaks to her: "Here, my queen. The others tried to steal it, knowing it was worth a small fortune. They tried to convince me by saying that we could all run away with it and start new lives with the money. That me and my family could live well for the rest of our lives. But I fought them for it, it wouldn't have been right to steal. You are not Sampson. You have done me no wrong, furthermore, you put yourself in harm's way to save my life, so my life was owed to you. I am not proud that I had to fight my friends and countrymen, but I am proud I stood up for what I felt was right. Here, my queen, here is your property. Myself and my family thank you for sparing my life earlier. Now, I must go." He hands her the pouch, and she opens it to see if the scissors are really there. And there they are, made of pure gold and diamonds. Solid gold scissors with diamonds embedded in the handles. She is saved. She sits on the floor for a moment, almost crying in her relief, and looks up to thank the servant, but he is gone. She snaps out of her momentary glee, and heads back to the bedroom. There is still work to be done, but now, she was armed.

She walks down the corridors, making sure no one else sees her, they might stop her and make noise, waking up Cain. She sees the dark sky start to lighten. Daybreak is no more than an hour away. She makes it to the bedroom door, and hopes she does not open it and see Cain awake. What will she do if she walks in, and he is standing there, next to the door, waiting for her? What if she walks in, and he wakes up, or if he is already awake, sitting up in bed, angry because she is not there? She knows she has to cast aside all her fears, and open that door. She didn't close the door completely when she left, so all she has to do is lightly push it to reenter. She pushes the door, and peeks her head in. Cain is still fast asleep. All her worries were for nothing. Now, it was time.

She carefully walks back to the bed, and crouches down next to his side. He had been lying down facing her earlier, so now his hair flowed off the edge of his bedside. She reaches into the pouch and draws out her weapon. The blade is long, but not long enough to cut all of his hair at once without her bunching it together in her hands first. Would he wake up if she grabbed it? Does he have some kind of internal warning to protect the source of his Nightmare power? She figures that grabbing his locks would be too risky. Instead, she was going to just cut the hair as it lay. It would take a few snips, but she felt it would cause no trauma to his head, waking him up. If she has his hair in her hands, and he was to move, it would surely yank and wake him up. Yes, this way was no doubt

safer. She puts the scissors next to his hair, opens them up, and goes to cut, hoping it cuts clean and sharp. With what can only be described as magical, the scissors cut through his hair before she even closes them. Without a hint of noise, the hair touches the blade and falls from his head, then, instantly vanishes into thin air. At first, she stopped, caught off guard by the way the scissors worked, but she realizes that the Overseer made sure she had to right tool for the job. In the dreamscape, many things seem as if they are items of magic, nothing is impossible. And the Overseer obviously had the means to send magical objects into the real world.

Quickly, she glides the blade across his locks as if she were moving the blade through air. There was no resistance at all, she never felt a single strand. With no effort, she has robbed the Nightmare of all his power. With one stroke, he was nothing more than mortal. Now, he had to suffer his mortal death. Now, her fear was gone, and was replaced by sorrow. She knows that even if he were to wake up, he would be no match for her now. She still had the power of the Daydreamers, while he had none. She moved quietly, so that he would not suffer, so he would die in his sleep. She stood above him, ready to cut his throat, when the Overseer's voice rings loudly in her mind. "The heart! CUT OUT HIS HEART WHILE IT STILL BEATS AND CRUSH IT IN YOUR HANDS!! So speaks the Overseer."

She knows she cannot question the Overseer, she has no choice. The tears start to fall from her eyes as she holds the blade over his heart. He lay there asleep, with a small smile on his face, and now, she must betray and butcher him. She holds the scissors over his chest, and plunges them downward.

Again, penetration is achieved without resistance, but this time, Cain does react. Cain's eyes pop open as he looks at her, startled, confused. "Till death do us part, my love....and so, we part" she speaks with tears running down her face." Quickly, she finishes the job before he could try to run from her, making him suffer more. She just wanted this to be over, to end any pain he might be in. She cuts a huge circle around his heart, and rips it out of his body. She holds his beating heart in her hands, and looks into Cain's eyes as he dies his mortal death. She can see the sorrow in his eyes, she can see the question "Why?" in the way he looks at her. He dies with the same expression on his face, staring at her, he will not blink, he can not blink. She feels the anger and pain inside of her; she feels so used. "WHY?? WHY??," she sobbed. Crying out in sorrow, she crushes the heart in her hands. Again, the Overseer speaks to her mind. "Well done, little one. Now dismember the carcass and rejoin our realm. All must see the true vulnerability of man."

She asked the question why, and didn't understand that the Overseer just reminded her and answered it. Man had to see that no mortal is invulnerable. If Sampson were allowed to live, the view of mortal man would have forever been distorted and tainted. Sampson had to die, and he had to die at the hands of a woman. So now to the task of the carving. "One piece at a time", the Overseer bellows. "One finger at a time, one toe, then the hands, feet, etc.", the voice rings in her mind, and she knows she must hurry. She reaches up and closes Cain's eyes; she can't do this while his dead eyes stare at her. She closes his eyes and grabs one of his hands to start the carving. She glides the scissors across one of his fingers, it falls off, and

then she is startled as she hears a blood-curdling scream in her head. *IT'S CAIN! HIS SOUL IS STILL TRAPPED IN HIS BODY! HE CAN FEEL THIS! NO!!! NO!!!!! I CANT DO THIS! I CANT DO THIS!!!!* "Calm yourself, little one. This is the first stage of sentence for the Nightmare. I have forced his soul to remain in his body, so that he will feel what countless others have felt due to his carnage. Thousands of mortals have died at his hands, and many of those have suffered greatly in doing so. You are not evil at heart, this does not come easy to you, but whether you understand or not, nonetheless, THIS IS JUSTICE! Now, carry out the sentence."

Assante takes a deep breath to gather herself, then proceeds to finish. Slice after slice, she dismembers his body, hearing his screams as she tears him apart. She tries to block out the his agony, but she can't. She just speeds up to get it over with. The faster she gets it done, the faster his soul can leave this body, and the sooner she can leave the plane of reality and go back to the dreamscape. One piece at a time, as commanded, she slices him up, but it only takes a couple of minutes. With the magic scissors, flesh and bone just fall away like butter. Soon, it's all over. She stands there, looking at the bloody scene, his beautiful body barely recognizable. She can't stand to look anymore, and just then, she hears voices approaching. Time for him to be found, and time for her to leave. Quickly, she dissipates into the coming dawn's light. Her job is done.

The Overseer pulls Cain into his realm. Cain rises through the cloudy floor, still disoriented from his ordeal. "Cain Nightmare, you have been tried and found guilty of a crime. You have knowingly and willingly used your abilities to warp the way man would perceive himself, thus mistreating the healthy evolution of the race. You will now be sentenced." Cain hears the Overseer's voice, calm, rational, as if he is not at all bothered by the pain and torture he just made him endure. All he can think about is the betrayal he just experienced; anger and pain fill inside of him. "To hell with you, you think I give a damn about what you think or say. I got other shit on my mind. Look, do what you gotta do, I don't care anymore." Cain speaks out of pure anger. He doesn't even stop to ponder the disparity of his current position.

"Cain, the betrayal you have experienced is but the first part of your sentence, the remainder is to be served throughout the remainder of man's of existence. Our assassin has delivered you back to this court, and here is where you will pay the price for your crime. You tried so hard to ruin man, now, you will serve him."

"Wait, you mean you set me up? The girl was sent by you?!"

"Yes, Nightmare, the girl was one of us, the Daydreamer, Assante. She volunteered for the task, and fulfilled her obligations to the letter of the court. She carved the body you held so dear, into little pieces. Even now, the children of the men you have killed are lining up to collect pieces of your body as trophies. The stories of your brutal murder at the hands of a woman are already being spread as fast as the storytellers can speak. The great Sampson was mutilated by a single woman. Now what mortal man would worship that? All you have done, has been undone. You shall go down in history as a fool." Cain now understands and shifts the focus of his anger more towards the Overseer, rather than on Assante. He

knows of the power the Overseer, he knows that once a deal had been made, no matter what, Assante had to finish it. Even though she ripped his heart from his body, he felt it was her heart to take anyway. He has feelings for her. He tells himself that she was just a pawn to the Overseer. To justify the longing he feels for Assante, he tells himself that she too, was setup, and tricked into the task she was sent to complete. Now, his anger was totally focused on the Overseer. "If you're so all powerful, show your ass so I can rip your fuckin' heart out!! I swear, if I ever get a chance for revenge, I'll redefine the word **suffer**. It could be a thousand years from now, but believe me, it's gonna be a retroactive ass kickin'! I'm going to remember this here shit, you fuckin' coward, you better believe that!"

"QUIET!!!!," the Overseer bellows, "you will now be sentenced so that I may be through with you! Cain Nightmare, for your crime you will no longer hold the title as Nightmare. However, the balance in the dreamscape must be maintained. There must always be a male and female Daydreamer and Nightmare. Thus, Shoma, the male Daydreamer will assume the role of the male Nightmare. He will evolve as of now to posses all the power and abilities you have so foolishly squandered away. You will be demoted to that of a Daydreamer. You will no longer walk amongst man at night; at night you will serve the human race. You will no longer be blessed with the ability to assume any form you wish. You will be confined to mortal shapes. You will, however, keep your heterosexual orientation, and will not be able to change it. You are now, and will forever be heterosexual as part of your sentence. Your power levels are hearby diminished, and your first night's work awaits you. Now, be gone."

Suddenly, Cain wakes up in the dreamscape as if he had been asleep. He looks around at his surroundings. He is in a Roman coliseum. And he is in the garb of a warrior. *How far in time was I sent?* Time is not a factor in the dreamscape. Elderly people dream themselves as young; many people have dreams of the future, others have dreams of the distant past. There is no true time continuum in the dreamscape. So now, Cain finds himself in the time where the Romans ruled.

There he stands, in the coliseum, and the crowd is chanting in unison, "Fight, Fight, Fight!" He wonders, *who is the dreamer here? Who's the subject?* Then, a lone warrior walks into the scene and the crowd roars. Cain looks at the warrior. There is nothing special about him, he stands about 5'10" tall, weighs about 190 pounds. No big deal, though, because whoever dreamed him on this night, made him a superior male. He stands a good 6'8" and is very muscular, a role he has well adapted to. He figures the warrior in front of him surely isn't the dreamer. So he does what he does naturally, and what the crowd is cheering for: he fights. Quickly, he kills the warrior and raises his hands up in victory. Warrior after warrior, turn into corpse after corpse. Cain is having a ball, he is letting out all the pent up aggression he felt towards the Overseer. Each death he deals is more and more bloody, a massacre. His favorite means of death seems to be ripping out the hearts of the warriors with his bare hands, and crushing them in his hands as he raises them it to the crowd. Each time, a crowd roars with excitement and cheers. *This is great!*, he thinks to himself. *If this is my punishment, if this is my sentence, then this is going to be a blast.* " Bring it on, give me MORE!," he yells. Next, lions are released into the forum, and again, he rips them apart with his bare hands. None can stand against him. He is the strongest man in Rome.

Finally, all the fighting stops. No challengers remain, and he is declared the victor over all. He takes his bows, and basks in the moment of worship from the crowd as they exit the coliseum. Then the scene changes, he is suddenly naked in what seems to be the shower area. His hands and body bloody from the victims' blood, he figures he's supposed to wash it off, why else would he be here. As he washes his body down, he thinks aloud, "I don't get it. Ok, wait, lemme think about this, I just don't get it. Who was the dreamer? Is this someway different the Daydreamer's work? Do I never get to meet the dreamer? Was it someone in the crowd that just wanted to see a fight? I mean, it was fun and all, but what was the point? Man, this is confusing. Guess I'll just wash up and wait and see what happens next." As he starts to rinse the soap from his body, he hears the sound of hands clapping nearby. It's the sound of one person, and he turns, gazing through the steam to see who is applauding. It is Emperor Caesar. He approaches Cain in his famous white toga, and gold leaves in his hair. "Great battle today, my warrior." Caesar stands there, looking at Cain. Cain figures it was Caesar that dreamt him, that he wanted to see a unbeatable warrior. Ok, this was good. He thinks, *Oh, ok, now it makes sense. Caesar is a conqueror. He probably dreamed me unbeatable, and is now going to send me out to war to win him more empires. Ok, more killing, I have no problem with that, I'll will be worshiped as a warrior, he will be worshiped as an emperor. Fair enuff. Lemme play into this.* Cain is unaccustomed to being a Daydreamer, normally a Daydreamer would just read the mind of the dreamer and

ascertain his needs. But this was Cain's first night on the job. He had psychic abilities as a Nightmare, but he rarely used them. He never cared what was on the minds of others, he was always in it for himself. So now, he just guessed as best he could as to the meaning of the dream, and Caesar's visit. "Thank you, Emperor, I live to serve Rome, and of course its emperor, Caesar. Anyone that will defy the will of Caesar is my blood enemy, and I vow myself against all such fools!"

"Very good, my willing warrior, very good. You live to serve Rome and its emperor you say?"

"Absolutely!"

"Then serve me, warrior, serve me now! Lend your body to the needs of your emperor." Cain is puzzled by the request. He thinks, *What in the hell is he talking about? Lend my body to him, serve him now? What does he want me to do? How can I serve him now, there is no one here to kill.* Just then, Cain's train of thought is broken by the touch of Caesar grabbing his dick from behind him.

"I am Caesar, I conquer all. I shall conquer the strongest man in Rome! I am Caesar, you will know that I am THE STRONGEST MAN IN ROME, SLAVE!"

Oh, hell no! HAS HE LOST HIS FUCKIN' MIND? Caesar IS GAY! NO WAY! Well, it doesn't matter, his dumb ass dreamed me being way stronger than him, I'll just kill him as I killed the rest. No big deal. As Cain turns to grab the neck of Caesar, then rip his heart from his body, the true penalty of the Overseer shows itself. The main difference between Daydreamers and Nightmares is control. A Nightmare has control over itself in the dreams, Daydreamers don't. A Daydreamer's body is connected to the mind of the dreamer. They are no

more than living puppets, whose strings are pulled at will by the people who dream about them. This fact is made readily apparent as he turns to face Caesar. "Up against the wall, SLAVE!" As Caesar speaks the words and pushes Cain in the back, Cain is forced face first into the shower wall. Cain has lost all use of his body, his hands are outstretched in front of him now, with his palms flat against the wall. He can't control his legs, which are being spread apart by Caesar. His body feels like a prison, he can't control his mouth or his words. Whatever Caesar wants him to do, he does. His body reacts from the pure thought of Caesar. Without warning, he hears himself uttering words, "Please, my lord, spare me, I bow to you Lord Caesar", only to hear Caesar bark back, "Shut up, slave. You're lucky I consider you good enough to fuck. Tell me, slave, tell me how lucky you are! Tell me how you are privileged to be fucked by Caesar!" Cain struggles with every fiber of his being, but to no avail. He feels his mouth open and the words come out. "Yes, Caesar, I am lucky. I am lucky to have you want me. You are all powerful, I bow to your power and ask you to fuck me, my lord. I belong to you." If he could throw up, he would. He is in pure torture as he feels the dick of Emperor Caesar sliding up his ass. With all the chaos going through his mind, he hears a piercing laugh. It's the Overseer, he is busting a gut, laughing at Cain. Watching him be raped. Now he understood how keeping his heterosexual orientation was part of his punishment. He had not factored in the gay population. As a Nightmare, he was able to reject such dreamers. But now, for eternity, he was going to submit to all. And as a heterosexual, he would never enjoy any aspect of male-to-male experience. But this was his sentence, for the rest of man's existence. As he thought deep about what lie before him, he felt his body moving. *Oh, no* he thought. *No*! He felt his hands leave the wall and open his ass up for Caesar. Then he felt Caesar enter him, hard and fast. He couldn't move away, he couldn't slide forward to ease the blow, he just took it. To make matters worse, Caesar dreamed himself with a huge dick, and he made Cain scream out like a virgin woman! The rape was long and painful, Caesar made sure he dreamed it that way. What else would a gay conqueror dream of? Of course he would have dreams of conquering the strongest man alive, and Caesar was in total domination of Cain. Over and over Caesar would slap Cain in the face while he raped him, demeaning him verbally while he assaulted his body. "Now, slave, suck my dick!," Caesar shouted. Cain wanted to die, he wished he could kill himself right then and there. He felt his knees bending. He couldn't stop himself. His mouth opened, and he grabbed Caesar's dick, and put it in his mouth. In his head, he heard the continuous laughter of the Overseer. From the start of the rape, the laughter never stopped, it just got louder and louder. Caesar was slapping Cain in the face while he pleased him. Cain wanted to bite down on Caesar so badly, but his mouth wouldn't close. His head just went back and forth, and Caesar kept slapping him, "Faster, slave, faster! Can't you do anything right! Make me cum you fuckin' slave. Make me cum!" Cain knew Caesar was ready to cum, he felt Caesar's dick grow larger, and he felt Caesar's veins rising in his mouth. Caesar commanded, "Now swallow, me slave! Swallow me!" Then Caesar came, and it was violent, right down his throat, choking Cain, and he kept cumming, in unreal amounts, but it was his dream. Caesar wanted him to choke.

Then Caesar pulled his dick out and came all over Cain's face, using his dick to spread it around his cheeks and neck. All the time, the music in Cain's tortured mind was that of the Overseer's inane laughter. The rape was complete, but before it was all over, Caesar made Cain use his fingers to wipe the cum from his face and neck, and lick it off his fingers. For Cain, this was worse than a thousand deaths. It was finally over as he felt himself being pulled into another dream, this time, one with a woman. He welcomed the change, like water being poured on a burning fire in his soul. He knew he would have to do what she commanded of him; he would never again have free will in the dreamscape. As far as women were concerned, he knew he could deal with that just fine, he could learn to like it. But with the men, oh no, he had to find revenge. He contemplates how to exact revenge on Caesar. *Caesar's ass gotta pay for this! Ok, I can't walk amongst the mortals at night anymore, I'm a fuckin' Daydreamer now, I will be amongst them during the day. That's when I'll get him. What can I do? What's the best way to get back at a man? I have to attack his manhood as he attacked mine. What to do, what to do.............oh, I GOT IT! Caesar has a wife, the most beautiful woman in Rome. I'll fuck her, and make Caesar see me. Nothing can be worse to a man than watching another man come and fuck your woman. And with the ego of a conqueror, it will tear him apart! That's it! That's my revenge! Killing him would be too easy, he must live to suffer, as I will live to suffer."*

Dawn arrives....and Cain appears in the realm of the real earth. He chooses the guise of the warrior/slave Caesar dreamed. *The man in his dreams will betray him. That will stop him from dreaming about me again. It will free me from his dreams as well as serve as my revenge. This is perfect.* So he stands outside the gates of the Roman coliseum. He pounds on the doors. "Let me in, I wish to fight for the Emperor and patrons of Rome!" The huge double doors open, and in he walks, just as in the dream. He is strong, but not as strong, or invulnerable as in the dreams. He has to make it a good show, plus, he doesn't want to invoke another punishment from the Overseer. Being too strong is what got him into trouble in the first place. Still, with the limited power he uses, he defeats all challengers. Caesar's wife, who is drawn to power in a man, is instantly drawn to his strength, and summons one of the guards over to her. She whispers in the guard's ear, "After the contest, bring that warrior to my private chamber." The guard nods, understanding the need for secrecy, and walks downstairs towards the arena area. Cain is just finishing up his last competition and walks off to the roar of the crowd. He enters the exit tunnel where the guard intercepts him. "Excuse me stranger, but the Emperor's wife wishes to discuss a matter of great secrecy with you. Please, follow me, if you will." Cain knows that his ploy has worked, and his revenge is near. Cracking a sarcastic smile, he says "Of course I will, I'll do anything to serve Rome and my empress." The guard escorts him to the private quarters high on the fifth floor of the coliseum and closes the door behind him.

"You have fought great battles on this day, warrior. Do you have any energy left for your empress?" Caesar's wife slips out of her clothes, and approaches Cain. "I am a Warrior of Rome, I live to serve. I will gladly lay down my life for Rome, and just as eagerly lay down its Empress." Cain sweeps

her off her feet, and goes to work. Quickly, he takes her to the wall, just as he did Assante. The last time he was with a woman of his own free will, he was with Assante, and this was his way of reliving his last happy moments, a way to hold on to what was, and will never be again. The sex is primal and raw, just as with Assante, until, with his heightened sense of hearing, he hears Caesar approaching. He knows it's time for the one moment of revenge. He wants Caesar to see his wife in the most submissive of positions. As Caesar nears the door, Cain forces the empress on her knees so that he may cum on her, the same way Caesar came on him. And true to the script in Cain's mind, just as Caesar opened the door, he came all over her face. Caesar stood there in the doorway, shocked, stunned, and Cain just held her head, and used his dick to smear it all over her face and neck. The revenge was complete, and Cain looked down at her face, then looked over at Caesar, made eye contact, and smiled.

Caesar quickly called for the guards to come and seize Cain. "Guards!! Guards!! Seize him and take him to the dungeon. His life will be forfeit tomorrow!" 6 guards came to drag Cain away, but he offered no resistance. He just walked out with them, laughing all the way. It was the best of all situations, he was to be killed the next day, but he knew he would dissipate by nightfall. He wouldn't even have to suffer the whole bothersome, mortal death thing. He would just go down to this dungeon, and wait it out. Nightfall was only about 3 hours away anyway. As he is lead past Caesar, Cain yells out, "Have any good dreams lately, Caesar??" And he's led away, laughing the whole way.

In the dungeon, he awaits nightfall. He's there about an

hour when he hears what he assumes to be a guard coming his way. He can't turn to see who it is because he's shackled facing the wall. So he just waits to see who it is. A few moments pass, then he feels someone standing behind him, and grab his dick. It's Caesar. *Oh no, NOT AGAIN!!* Cain thought. In his inexperience in being a Daydreamer, and his blind desire for revenge, he had not fully thought through his plan. He arrived in the same guise as Caesar's dream warrior, and proved himself to be the strongest man in Rome. On top of that he gave Caesar a motive for revenge, and now was shackled head and feet, against a wall. Of course Caesar would come for him! He felt Caesar rub his dick up against him as he did in the dream. "You will die with my cum in your ass, you fuckin' slave!" And Cain knew there was nothing he could do. He could easily break the chains and kill Caesar, but that would be a display of strength too great. It would break the laws that got him this sentence in the first place. No, he had made a dire mistake. *Not again!*, he thought. *Not again, No way!! He's gonna fuck me again! Damn you, Caesar! Damn you!!!* But he didn't voice it, he didn't give Caesar the pleasure of hearing him scream. While Caesar raped him, Cain just remembered the confinements of his sentence, "I must serve man for the duration if his existence." Now Cain knew he could not forcefully kill Caesar, but he could change his own blood and excretions, and make Caesar sick. As he was in the middle of being raped, he came to the realization that he must serve man until man dies out. Thinking of the millions of nights to come where he will be raped over and over again by the gay population, with no free will of his own, and being locked into this heterosexual orientation, he makes Caesar sick. He causes an

illness to spread to Caesar, which Caesar will pass on each time he takes another, and they will pass it on, and so on, and so on. "On this day, I give to you, my gift. Any man, who takes a man will die a slow, painful death. The plague will spread like wildfire, and there will be no cure, only death. You will be married to my plague, til death do us part." Cain has finally found his revenge, and maybe a way to shorten his sentence. "If I must serve man for the duration of his existence, let the men who crave men carry the plague that will shorten their very existence, and free me from my hell, so speaks Cain." To this day, the AIDS virus plagues the planet. It affects millions of men and women. Once again, out of anger, Cain didn't think it through. But neither did Caesar.

The Daydreamers walk amongst us......were you nice to the lover in your dreams?

JUICY

I have an insatiable thirst,
It courses though my veins.
A thirst for pure passion,liquid lust,
And now, it has a name.

Her moniker, is Juicy,
The very definition of wet.
Primal Lust, Dripping electricity,
This is the woman I have to get.

To milk her body, with my tongue,
To lick her lips, for her prize.
To hold her cum, in my mouth,
Not swallowing, til she looks in my eyes.

Ohh I yearn for all that she is,
Because she's much more than what you see.
She is the wet, that's in my dreams.
She is the fire, that is my desire.
ALL my yearnings now have a name,
And her moniker,
Is JUICY.

PLEASE

You sit on the bed, legs open,
"Nigga beg for this pussy if you want some!"
I crawl on the floor on my stomach,
"Please baby, can I make you cum?"

Inch by inch, I'm crawling closer,
Scratching, yearning, just to get a taste.
I ask for authorization to satisfy you,
I plead for permission, "Please fuck my face!"

My tongue is right next to your smooth, wet clit.
If I don't get a lick, I'm gonna die!
I tongue fuck you first, then slide up to your spot,
But before I proceed, "Baby, may I?"

You turned me into your *tramp* baby,
You got me on my knees.
I'll be your damn *fuck-slut* lover,
"May I please you now, baby.....Please???"

FUCKTIVITY

Level One
Just barely "gettin' sum"
Ya can hardly say ya "hit!"
He didn't lick da pussy,
She didn't suck da dick.

Level Two
When ya glad it's ova, happy it's through!
"Damn baby, you wasn't even wet!"
"Fuck you nigga! Is that as hard as you can get?!"

Level Three
At this level you can both agree,
That the sex was weak, but you'll say it's fine,
But not worth doing again, not really worth the time.

Level Four
You did once, maybe once more.
Was the pussy too loose??? Too close ta make a call.
Or the nigga can work it some, but the dick...was kinda small.

Level Five
Finally some sex worth the time!
Basic, but good, finally, you both came!
When you tell your friends how it was, both your stories will be the same.

Level Six
From here on, it's all good pussy and good dicks!
She's got control of them pussy muscles,
And the dicks are long and thick.

Level Seven

Feels like heaven,
long tongue massages on the clit,
And when she sucks it, she swallows every dayum inch on the dick!

Level Eight

Oh, are they the perfect mates??!!!
The sex is impeccable, you can't believe your luck!
You call in sick to work, just so you can stay home and fuck!

Level Nine

Where the perfect lays, are perfectly fine.
No place on woman's body can you find a flaw,
And the men are all ripped, hung, and tall!

LEVEL TEN

The ultimate in sex, the epitome of sin!
When ya cum till ya sore! Beggin' for Pleasure, Pleading for Pain!
Even on a Sunday, you're screaming the Lord's name out in vain!!!

So these are the levels of Fucktivity.
Choose whichever one fits your form.
My level, you ask??? Well, let's call it Eleven,
So consider yourself warned!

PAYBACK

I was your bitch,
You had total control of my ass!
Until you got weak and had mercy,
Then I dropped you to the floor,
Hard, Strong, and Fast!

Next time you try to own me,
Don't save nuthin', ya betta bring it all.
If you don't I'll be fuckin' your hot, shakin' body,
Or stickin' a dick down your throat,
So no one can hear you call.

Yeah, you thought that shit was fun, huh?
Makin' me beg, eat, and heel!!
An Owner-Bitch relationship, it was simple,
Then you got all soft, and broke the deal.

Someone musta told yo' dumb ass wrong,
When they said this was a game intended for play.
Cause I got ya knees on ya ears,
And I hear ya say you're scared,
All I can tell you is, lay down, shut up, hold on, and pray!

Cause you done pissed this ex-bitch off,
The passive shit is ova, I'm on the attack!
Reality's a bitch, Life's a bitch, and I used ta be yours too,
But the biggest bitch of all,
is PAYBACK!!!

ISSUES

Everybody got issues baby,
Everybody got loose ends.
We all done a lil' sumpin' wrong,
But what are *you* doing to make amends!?

What are *you* doing to make things better?
What are *you* doing to move ahead?
What are *you* doing to get rid of old issues?
And get a better man in your bed!

Not that a man is the root to all issues,
Cause I know a good one can help them go away.
You got the looks *and* mind to pull a good man,
But old-ass issues, will drive him away!

Issues only have power if you let them,
They can come between a good woman and a good man.
But with two hearts that care,
Life's burdens are shared,
Tackling those issues hand in hand.....
Understand?!

Busted

I came home early, as a suprise,
And saw you and him lying in our bed.
I wondered what you done to him,
Visions of you giving him head.

You lay there in his arms,
I know that grin, you just got you some.
I can see the sweat on the pillows,
and how the sheets were wet with your cum.

I gotta get this outta my mind,
I ain't that hard, I ain't gonna lie.
Cause if I think too hard on this here subject,
both your asses gotta die.

I ain't bullshittin'
I dont play dat shit.
I hope ya asked yourself before ya fucked him,
Is my life worth a dick??

So there y'all lay before me,
Recovering, not a worry in the least.
When you shut your eyes and laid down,
Did ya know, this might be your last piece?

I feel that anger building up,
I see the KY laying next to the glass.
Oh shit, now it's on!
I know he fucked you in the ass!!!

Why, oh why, did ya give him the ass, baby?
That was the last and final straw!
I can see revenge, redemption, and retaliation,
But right now, I can't see the law.

I'm about ta set it off,
Y'all bout ta learn the meaning of fear.
You was fuckin' anotha nigga,
Dat's why ya didn't want no guns up in here.

But I was brought up old school,
So I stashed one anyway.
For the simple fact that I hadta see this shit,
Both y'all bout ta pay.

But as I crept my way to the closet,
On the top shelf, where I hid my gun.
I heard him scream, "Your man is home!"
"Dat's right nigga, you betta run!!"

You jumped outta bed cryun,
"Wait baby, lemme explain!"
My advice to you all, in this situation,
Don't fuck with a brotha when he's insane.

Cause I shoved you to the floor,
then pointed the gun at your dome.
"How in the hell can you fuck anotha nigga!"
"And fuck him in my home!!!!!"

But then I heard him running,
So I chased, bustin' caps along the way.
Shooting in any direction,
Ain't no way he gonna get away.

As he reached the stairs,
So did I.
"You ain't goin' no where, nigga,
So don't even try!"

"Calm down man, I'm sorry"
"No one needs ta get hurt"

"Get your punk ass upstairs!"
"I'm about ta put in work!"

I had y'all both in the bedroom,
I made you get on your knees.
With my gun cocked and loaded,
"Now beg for your lives, ya betta plead!"

As I listened to y'all whimper,
Just gettin' off on your sorry sounds.
I hear the door get kicked in behind me,
"Yo, nigger...put the gun down!!"

Damn, someone called the cops,
I bet it was your nosey bitch across the street.
She knew you was here fuckin' around,
She knew some asses was gonna get beat.

"Put the gun down now or I'll kill ya"
The cop shouted as more entered the door.
"I shoulda shot ya when I had the chance"
And I dropped the gun to the floor.

They slammed me down hard,
Put a knee in my neck.
Cuffed my hands behind my back,
"Get your ass up, roughneck!"

So they dragged me to the car,
and carted me off to jail.
Put me up for attempted murder,
Set a million dollas bail.

I was guilty of course,
Sentenced to 20 years behind bars.
While she's still fuckin' that nigga in my bed,
and I know he's drivin' my dayum car!

But I tell myself I asked for it,
And this is the price I gotta pay.
If you have any conflict in your life, deal with it,
Trust me, violence ain't the way.

I'll spend the next 20 years locked up,
Over a bitch that shoulda never been trusted.
I thought *I* was slick, I thought *they* were caught,
But *I'm* the one that ended up **BUSTED**.

1 Week Made Me 2 Weak

I stood before the Lord,
Proclaimed my love til death do us part.
I'd give my life for you,
As I've given you my heart.

My love was so complete that day,
As you'd given me your hand.
But your heart was secretly breaking,
For the love, of my best man.

The day after you accepted my proposal,
You and him, shared your honeymoon.
I used to pray for life to be long and happy,
Now death, can't come too soon.

One week after I said I do,
I'm screaming in pain, ***"How could you??!!"***
As the truth of your betrayal came out in time,
That the child you would give me, isn't really mine.

One week was the duration of the rest of my life.
One week til death do us part, one week you were my wife.
I feel my soul leaving me, finally, my agony is through!
Guess I was too weak to live with the truth,
And too weak, to live without you.

Thank you

I would like to thank

God for my creation, my talent, and all the blessings I have received in my life.
My Mom and my Dad for all your sacrifice and love. I could not have dreamed for better parents in life. The love and dedication you have shown to each other, has been a model example of marriage and family. I thank God for you every night, and I love you more than words can say.
Franny for believing in me more than anyone ever has, without you baby, this book or company would have never happened.
Vella, my sister, for loving and protecting me as a child. All the flowers I picked for you through the years, can never repay the debt.
Prince, for being so damn funky! The very first slow dance I ever had was to, "When we're dancing close and slow". When I held a girl for the first time, and heard you say, "I can almost taste the thoughts within your mind." That one line, that one moment, opened up the part of me that would yearn to articulate the true essence of the emotions I would enjoy and endure in my life. Thank you.
Cynthia, my cousin, girl, you just silly, but you've been good to me my whole life. **Billy** her husband, be good to her.
Anthony my cousin, I've watched you grow from a baby to a man. You were always a good kid, now be a strong and good man. I've needed your youthful humor and energy to keep me going. I love you dawg.
DL, owner of Tangles and Locks. You have always been more than a barber to me. You've been a real and true friend. I respect your accomplishments, and your determination. There are not a lot of barber shops around anymore that have a sense of family, where black men and women can gather just to talk and have fun in peace. Tangles has always been extended

family to me, thank you for providing such a healthy atmosphere, and for always showing your fellow man and woman love.
Ika, my fellow general. Thank you for the short years we kicked it. I will always look back on those nights clubbin' together, night after night, after night, without rest, as one of the best times in my life. That time came at a vital point in my life, you kept me true to myself. Oh, and thank you for being the only brotha I know who can walk in a club in a mustard suit and sunglasses, and pull women like crazy. COURAGE ......a true playas most vital tool.
Tricia, the first woman in my life, who was really "the one". The level of love and heartbreak I have endured over you has made me a whole person. Proof positive that what is not meant to be, will not come to pass. No matter how hard I tried to will it, God's plan can not be changed.
Nene, for being my first love.
Sharise, for being my first experience with a true dog.
To: **Pam, Veronica, Allison, Bunny, Kamila, Krystal, Valerie, Jamie, Tye, & Vaurlon**. In one way, shape, or form, you've all contributed in part to the man I am today.
Chris, my web page designer, maybe I shoulda e-mailed this thank you, then I know you woulda got it.
The members of **Troop - Jon Jon, Reggie, Allen, Steve, & Rodney**. Rodney, when we gonna ball? Jon, thanks for all those nights we kicked it and talked about our dreams coming true.
Dallas, my best friend in this world. I know I never get to see you, but you are always with me. There were many years in school as a child where you were my only friend. You never faltered in your role as my best friend, and I would have had many lonely years with no one to call a friend if you weren't there. I cant begin to tell you how much love I have for ya. Oh, Dallas, tell **Jerome, Eric, De Shawn, and Lerome** I said wuzzup, and thank you for all the good ol days playin' basketball in the driveway. And tell **Doug** I'm extremely proud of how he grew up, he's your brother, but I feel like he's mine too. Say a prayer for your mom, I thank her for taking me into her family, God rest her beautiful soul. And to your

dad,.......thank him for bein' so tolerant of all us crazy boys up in his house.
Kalonie, my homegirl, and my god-daughters mother. I've known you since I was 16, and you always been a good and true friend. But, girl...get them tubes tied or find you a man to marry, ya know!
Mao, my true partna. You still greedy when it comes to women dawg, dayum you greedy. But you are a true friend, and I thank you for always havin my back.
Lyssa, my flower child. Well, I don't know if all is good in the universe, but no matter how corrupt the world becomes, you will always be pure of heart in my eyes. Thank you for always being there for me to call in all hours of the night.
People I can't forget: **Mark, Ron, Vita, Pierre, Tyrone C., Nache, Reggie H. Nick, Michele, Joe & Spanky.**
"To all the people I have forgot, you can charge it to my head, and not my heart."

And thank you to all the people that have purchased this book. Thank you from the bottom of my heart for your support. Please, send in your ideas for the next books and products. *This company and myself are here to serve you all, we strive to provide what you really want, not force you to pick from what's available.*

Reach us via the internet at **www.wickedpleasures.com**
To order additional copies of this book or products call toll free ***1-877-2WICKED***
reach us via mail at:

<u>**Wicked Pleasures**</u>
P.O. Box 40279
Pasadena, CA 91114